PENGUIN BOOKS

# PEOPLE LIKE THEM

SAMIRA SEDIRA is a novelist, playwright, and actress who was born in Algeria and moved to France with her family when she was very young. In 2008, after two decades of acting for film and the stage, she became a cleaning woman, an experience that inspired her autobiographical novel *L'odeur des planches* (*The Smell of the Stage*). *People Like Them* is her fourth novel and the first to be translated into English.

LARA VERGNAUD is an award-winning translator who specializes in North African literature.

# People Like Them

**A Novel**

## SAMIRA SEDIRA

*Translated from French by*
**LARA VERGNAUD**

PENGUIN BOOKS

PENGUIN BOOKS
An imprint of Penguin Random House LLC
penguinrandomhouse.com

Originally published in French as *Des gens comme eux* by
Éditions du Rouergue, Rodez.

LIBRARY OF CONGRESS CATALOGING-IN-PUBLICATION DATA
Names: Sedira, Samira, author. | Vergnaud, Lara, translator.
Title: People like them : a novel / Samira Sedira ; translated from
French by Lara Vergnaud.
Other titles: Des gens comme eux. English
Description: New York : Penguin Books, [2021]
Identifiers: LCCN 2020049115 (print) | LCCN 2020049116 (ebook) |
ISBN 9780143136279 (paperback) | ISBN 9780525507871 (ebook)
Classification: LCC PQ3989.3.S44 D4713 2021 (print) | LCC
PQ3989.3.S44 (ebook) | DDC 842/.92—dc23
LC record available at https://lccn.loc.gov/2020049115
LC ebook record available at https://lccn.loc.gov/2020049116

Printed in the United States of America
1st Printing

Set in Stempel Garamond LT Pro • Designed by Sabrina Bowers

This is a work of fiction based on actual events.

*For my son*

*We cannot despair of humanity,*
*since we are ourselves human beings.*

—Albert Einstein, *The World As I See It*

# People Like Them

There's no cemetery in Carmac. The dead are buried in the neighboring towns. But animal corpses are allowed. At the foot of a tree or in the corner of a garden. Here, animals die where they lived. Men don't have such luck.

The small chapel overshadowed by a row of hundred-year-old plane trees doesn't have much use anymore. People take refuge there in the summer, when the air becomes unbreathable. A haven of silence, coolness, and shade. Inside, thanks to the cold, moist stones, it feels like breathing deep within a cave. In the month of August in Carmac, everything burns. The grass, the trees, the children's milky skin. The sun allows no respite. The animals drag, too; the cows produce less milk; the dogs sniff at their food, then return to the shade, nauseous.

In the winter, it's the opposite—everything freezes. Cloudy River, which crosses the valley, gets its name from that particularity: transparent and elusive in the summer, cloudy and iced over in the winter.

The village, built on either side of the river, is connected by a stone bridge called Two Donkeys Bridge. It has a grocer's store, a post office, a town hall, a small bus station, a bakery, a café, a butcher shop, and a hairdresser. There's also an old sawmill whose machines haven't whistled in more than twenty years. Now it serves as a hideaway for forest cats when it snows, or when the females give birth.

If you approach the village from the hillside road, it disappears into a vast pinewood, revealing its plunging valley only when you emerge from the last turn.

The most peaceful season here is autumn, when the western wind sweeps away the last of the summer heat. Beginning in September, the sharp air cleanses the stone and rinses the undergrowth. The valley finally breathes. The autumn purge. White, clear, unrebellious sky. All that remains is the fragrance of wet grass, a smell of the world's beginning with hints of pine resin. At dawn, the beams of the school bus announce a new day. Chilled, sleepy teens pile in. They'll follow the river for a few miles until the intersection, when, at the call of the town's first murmurs, the bus will change direction. It's the hour when the youngest go to the village school and the adults to work. There are only two families of farmers left; all the others commute every day.

Life is peaceful in Carmac, calm and orderly. But the most striking thing here, when winter arrives, is the silence. A silence that spreads everywhere. A tense silence in which the slightest sound stands out: the footsteps of a stray dog crackling over dead leaves, a pinecone tumbling onto dry needles, a famished wild boar digging feebly at the ground, the naked branches of a chestnut tree rattling against one another when the wind picks up or crows fly by . . . And even sounds from miles away can be heard here. At night, if you listen closely, you can hear the tumble of rocks the weary mountain drops into small turquoise lakes, as milky and murky as blind eyes.

When evening comes, when the smoke of fog intermingles with that of burned fields and outside everything retreats, the houses fill with noise. Conversations are held between one room and another, the workday recounted, voices swelling, rising above the gurgling of the dishwasher, the sizzle of onions, the cries of a child who's dreading bath time and the loneliness night brings.

Maybe it's because of that din that nobody heard anything the night they were killed. They say there were screams, gunshots, begging. But the chalet walls absorbed everything. Carnage behind closed doors. And nobody to save them. Yet outside, not the slightest breath of wind. Nothing but an interminable winter silence.

The first month I cried and couldn't stop. For a long time, I tried to understand what had happened. Even now, I keep going through the story from beginning to end, trying not to forget a single detail. Sometimes one piece of the story will stick in my mind, to the point where I'm not able to sleep for several nights in a row. A detail that I unwind, analyze, dissect until I go mad, and that slips through my fingers as soon as I'm about to pierce its secret. These ruminations always seem ordinary enough, no different than the previous ones—that's what I want to believe—but when night comes, they charge, the pain in the back of my head rousing my memories before casting me, alone, into a cold corner of the bed at dawn.

That's what happened last night: a question repeated without end, an unsolvable riddle that I turned over and over as the hours went clammily by. And yet this question that kept me awake all night, that I tirelessly picked at without finding an answer, had already been asked of you clearly enough, by the prosecutor in the courtroom:

*Why did you go to wash your hands in the frozen river after you butchered all the members of the Langlois family? It's more than five hundred yards from the crime scene. Why not use one of the many sinks in the house? Anyone else would have done so. It's logical. Anyone else would have used the sink in the bathroom or in the kitchen, or even the toilet! But not you. You ran like a lunatic, with no fear of being seen, and once you reached the river, you pummeled at the ice because, as you said in your deposition, you absolutely had to wash your hands. You have to admit that's a bit strange. Why did it have to be the river?*

Met with your hunted look, the prosecutor got annoyed. *Stop staring at me like that, please, Mr. Guillot, and answer!*

His voice naturally carried far; volume cost him no effort. Meanwhile you said nothing, just stared at him obstinately. Only your lips twitched.

Contradictory feelings waged war inside you: the

desire to speak led disastrously to the inability to formulate the slightest explanation. Cornered, you found no other way out but to smile dumbly. In reality, you had no answer to give him, and your muteness echoed like the desolation that follows a major disaster. For the first time since your trial began, I felt pity for you.

The prosecutor who had taken your reaction as a personal affront (no surprise there) immediately rose from his chair. *In your position, and for your sake, Mr. Guillot, I would abstain from smiling!*

His deep voice brimming with natural authority had exploded in a roar with those words, prompting everyone to sit up abruptly in their seats.

Your smile disappeared at once. The prosecutor swallowed before continuing. *You ran out—that's what you told the police officers—and, I'm quoting, "sprinted all the way to the river."*

The prosecutor then raised his arms, like he was being held at gunpoint, and curled his upper lip. *A sprint?!* He paused. *Who . . .* He paused again. *. . . sprints, in the middle of winter, with temperatures below freezing, to go wash their hands soaked in the blood of their own victims? What exactly were you running from?* Pause. He repeated, *What were you running from?*

He obviously wasn't expecting a response, seeing as

he stopped for a few seconds to gather his thoughts, and then said, without even glancing at you, *The river was frozen, but that didn't stop you, Mr. Guillot. You banged at the thick crust of ice like a madman, first with the butt of your rifle, then with your fists, until it yielded. There were four inches of ice! Four inches, can you imagine?! It takes some rage to break through four inches, and you had just murdered an entire family with a baseball bat! You hit at the ice so hard that your hands split, "gushing blood." Those are your words, are they not?*

The prosecutor approached the stand, slightly out of breath, arms hanging alongside his body.

He had his back to the members of the jury, who were listening raptly. The prosecutor knew that nothing he said would escape their attention, and that a single word could suffice to reverse their final decision. As a representative of the law, he was responsible for people's consciences.

He looked at you intently and then asked, *Do you remember what you said during your deposition?*

You shrugged, a little lost.

*All right, I'll tell you. You said:* "My blood mixed with their blood. I couldn't handle it."

The prosecutor shook his head, and with an air of feigned astonishment, he repeated, a little softer and overly articulating every word: *"My blood mixed with their blood. I couldn't handle it."*

At that exact moment, he let out a mean snicker. It was odd, inappropriate. He must have realized it because his cheeks reddened. To contain his embarrassment, he resumed immediately, pointing at you with one stiff jerk of his chin to bring the attention back to you. *And you added, to explain your revulsion, "I wasn't there with my wife the times she gave birth. I'm not comfortable in hospitals. When I see blood, I pass out."*

A long silence followed, filling the audience with a sense of dread and icy stupefaction. He had cornered you in a dead end. Trapped you like a rat. He couldn't believe you were the kind of man to be afraid of blood. To him, it was a strategy aimed at softening the jurors. How could someone who was capable of killing five people tremble at the sight of blood? It seemed ludicrous, unimaginable. And yet. You really were horrified by blood. You could never bear to see the smallest drop. When one of our daughters skinned her knee or hand, you'd be paralyzed, watching her whimper, incapable of the slightest movement, and you invariably ended up calling me to clean the wound. Later, a psychiatric expert will corroborate the idea that a fear of blood doesn't prevent someone from killing. *We've already seen soldiers head bravely to the front and faint at the slightest prick of a vaccine shot!*

But at this stage of the trial, nobody wanted to believe you. You gritted your teeth, head down, face pale.

Then, for some odd reason, the prosecutor abruptly turned toward me, as though I was a last resort. Clearly separating each word, he said, *For someone who can't handle the sight of blood, looks like you overcame your phobia easily enough.* Laughter in the room. He was staring at me, at least I thought so until I realized that in reality, he wasn't actually seeing me. His gaze had lingered at random, and unfortunately it was in my direction that it had stopped. In the confused state in which I found myself, I felt guilty, the same as you. As if the mere fact of being your wife automatically incriminated me. Tears rose to my eyes. The calm veneer I had managed to maintain until then, at the cost of considerable effort, had cracked like dead wood. I was nothing but a piece of trembling humanity. A murderer by proxy.

A murderer's wife is reproached for everything: her composure when she should show more compassion; her hysteria when she should demonstrate restraint; her presence when she should disappear; her absence when she should have the decency to be there; and so on. The woman who one day becomes "the murderer's wife" shoulders a responsibility almost more damning than that of the murderer himself, because she wasn't able to detect in time the vile beast slumbering inside her spouse. She lacked perceptiveness. And that's what will bring about her fall from grace—her despicable lack of perceptiveness.

The prosecutor finally looked away and stared at the ground, vaguely annoyed. His lips quivered. I thought I heard him mumble: *Keep going, keep going.*

It was as if everything that had been said up to then had suddenly brought about some great inner turmoil in him. His back slumped. The powerful man he had forced himself to appear to be gave way to an ordinary one, as disconcerted as anyone by the great mystery of human nature. He was standing in the middle of the courtroom, with everyone else seated, and I remember wondering, observing his black, perfectly polished shoes, if he had shined them himself or if someone had done it for him.

Later, during the trial (I can't remember the sequence anymore), the judge asked you to describe the night of the murders while trying not to forget anything. Everything. Everything that you'd already told the police. The facts, nothing but the facts.

The words didn't come out right away; they had to be knocked around, shoved forward. But as soon as they were freed, you let them leap out of you, cold, without any particular modulations or emotions. None of it seemed to concern you, as though someone else had done the dirty work. Or as though you were reading text from a teleprompter. Guided by that escapist logic, you let that "someone else" talk; the other, the true perpetrator. Later, the psychiatric expert called to the stand will explain that it's not your "conscious self" who killed. And to illustrate his point, he will cite Nietzsche: *"'I did that,' says my memory. 'I could not have done that,' says my pride."*

No, none of it seemed to concern you. The memory of your confession still goes with me everywhere, like a black cloud above my head. I remember every one of your words, in detail, every single hesitation:

*I grabbed the bat with both hands, like this, and I hit him hard behind the neck. The kid was having a snack at the big table, chocolate milk in a white bowl. A hard blow to the neck, like this, with both hands. I think that's when his baby teeth came out. . . . The police officers told me that they'd found two teeth between the floorboards. Baby teeth, they said. . . . His head . . . his head fell forward onto the table, it made a sound, a loud sound, a . . . terrible noise; the bowl fell, too, pieces all over the ground. I threw up the first time. I felt nauseous, couldn't hold it back. He died instantly, I swear. I'm saying that for the family. He didn't suffer, I swear. The oldest came down from her room, yelling. She wasn't happy. "What was that noise? Nono, what did you break now? I can never do my homework in peace!" She was waving her arms all over the place, annoyed. I ended up face-to-face with her in the living room. First she smiled. Odd, I thought, why is the kid smiling? And then, when she saw the blood on the hat, her eyes got black, black, and her mouth trembled. She looked around. "Where's Nono?" she asked. Her face was anxious, her eyes like a hunted animal's. . . . I didn't answer. That's when she saw him. His head on the table. The blood. The bowl on the floor. She understood. She said, crying, "What's wrong with Nono, why isn't he moving?" She lifted her arms, she said, "I didn't do anything, it's a joke, right, Constant, this is all a joke, isn't it?" Sorry, I . . . Are all these details useful? For the family, it . . .*

The judge encouraged you to continue with a nod.

*Okay, well . . . I . . . I was saying that she was crying and screaming, "Please don't, Constant, please, I want to see my mom, Mom, I want my mom." She repeated "Mom" over and over, like she'd lost her mind, over and over. I raised the bat, I threw up again. She didn't try to run, nothing, she just crossed her arms over her forehead, she crouched in front of me, and "Mom" again, "I want my mom" over and over. I closed my eyes so I could go through with it. I hit her. Again. And again. I . . . I opened my eyes, blood, lots of blood . . . she . . . she was dead. I threw up again. Then I went upstairs to find the third one. She was hiding in the bathroom between the toilet bowl and a small cabinet, sucking her thumb. I told her to come out, to turn around—she obeyed without crying, nothing. I raised the bat high, real high, then against the neck again. Dead on the spot, like the first one.*

*I threw up one last time, then I checked the time. Their parents would be back soon. I thought that it would be impossible with the bat, the dad was too strong. I ran all the way to my garage. I grabbed the rifle, a double-barrel, I loaded it, then I went back to their house. The street was empty. In that weather, not a soul. I waited for them, hiding behind the door. It got dark. In winter night comes on quick here. In the silence, the dead bodies next to me, I . . . I was scared. I could hear their breathing. A corpse doesn't breathe, I told myself, but nothing doing, I heard it. And the smell of blood . . . I almost threw up again, but I managed to keep it down that time.*

*Finally the sound of a motor. I recognized it; it was them. The car doors slammed. The mother came in first, with bags of groceries. "We're back, kids!" she said, the father behind her. I didn't stop to think. I kicked the door shut and I shot them from behind. Him first. Then her. They collapsed, without realizing anything, without even having the reflex to turn around. It was over. I looked at them and I couldn't move. I was trembling. That was the only thing I could do, tremble. I couldn't stop trembling. I thought it would never stop. I looked out the window. Nobody. Blood, on my hands, and a smell of . . . a smell . . . It was death. That's when I got the idea to go wash myself in the river. I wasn't thinking of the cold, or the ice, or the distance, or of anybody who might see me. I didn't think of any of that, just that I was trembling, and that my hands were covered in their blood, and that I had to get my legs to move so that I could run to the river and wash myself and . . .*

You didn't have time to finish. A great cry of despair and terror, followed by a horrendous thud, made everyone freeze. Sylvia's mother had just fainted in the courtroom. Her husband was straddling her, trying to revive his wife by caressing her forehead, as if that would suffice. That ridiculous position gave the scene a poignant theatricality, as if this man and woman, who in the space of one night had lost everything that had given meaning to their lives, were characters in a bad dream and we were their trembling audience. The trial was adjourned for the day, and I hurried home, head buried in a thick scarf, haunted by your words. That night, alone in my bed, wrestling with an onslaught of anxiety, I started awake at every hour, each time that endless cry in the courtroom echoing in my head.

It was during that awful night that I realized that you had become inseparable from me, because I had loved you once, and because the story of your life had joined the story of mine in a tragedy beyond repair.

verything began one Saturday in July 2015. It was a terrible year bookended by terrorist attacks, the televised images of which had plunged us into a state of utter shock. We watched them playing on a loop, stunned, unable to allow ourselves to believe them. In reality, fear was shaking our certainties along with our legs. For reassurance, we comforted ourselves with the idea that city life clearly wasn't for us and that we were very lucky to live where we lived.

Calm appeared to return with the arrival of summer. Giddy from the smell of freshly mown hay and whiffs of lilac, we hadn't anticipated or even imagined the pale horror into which we would be plunged again only a few months later. Not only were we living almost outside of the world, we were also deaf to its upheavals.

On that beautiful July Saturday, Simon and Lucie got married. The celebration took place in the courtyard of the family farm, in the shade of a large cedar tree, beneath the long, low branches that touched the ground. Simon and I go a ways back, and knowing he was settling down at nearly thirty-seven delighted me as much as it did his parents, who had been sporting silly, fragile smiles ever since the engagement was announced, seemingly in constant fear of him changing his mind, which would have forced them to cancel the wedding and send everyone home. Simon was an endearing man, but his juvenile, boorish personality had delayed his entrance into the adult world. Until that day, he had oriented his life along two major axes: one, his work on the farm alongside his father, which he took very seriously; and two, weekend binges with his friends in pubs blanketed in sawdust. For God knows what vague reason, he had always loathed the idea of married life, and his imagining of it verged on a prison-like hell.

Lucie, Simon's bride, had miraculously succeeded where so many others had failed. The way she went about it remains, for all of us, a huge mystery.

We had perfect weather, a day drenched in sunlight.

In the late afternoon, the men, drunk from the heat and brandy, had grabbed two castrated pigs from the trough where they were gorging themselves and released them between the tables. The enormous creatures had grunted and run in every direction, chased by a pack of children with mauve cheeks whose growing elation, fueled by the adults' laughter and shouting, gradually approached frenzy. In their anxious flight, the pigs had trampled by, snouts wet and smeared with fresh barley, knocking over everything in their path.

Simon's bride, who had been on the dance floor, face beaming, abruptly found herself on the ground, legs spread beneath her white dress, mowed down by one of the pigs. Her small feet sticking out from the taffeta spiked with dry burdock were bare, and her right big toe, shorter than the other four, was bleeding a little. She laughed, and hiccupped, and laughed again, her face crinkled, moving her head stupidly. Her mother, slurring from inebriation, and whose high bun was falling pathetically onto her forehead, leaned toward her and with one stretched-out hand begged her to get up, because *Lushie, c'mon, a bride down for the count don't look sho good!*

She didn't seem to know that at this stage of the party, everyone was mixing up everyone else amid a general gaiety, and that etiquette, disarmed at the first glass of champagne, had long fled the scene.

The bride wasn't the center of attention anymore despite the fact that she was slightly off-kilter and regularly getting twisted up in her long white veil. Even Simon himself was no longer focused on her. Standing on a chair before an exclusively male audience, he was chanting the chorus of *La Marseillaise*, one fist lifted toward the cedar tree's highest branches, and encouraging everyone to sing with him: *Aux armes citoyens, sortez vos aiguillons, fourrons, fourrons, qu'un blanc impur abreuve nos dondons!* It was a terrible concert of wrong notes, whistles, and hollers. Marie, the old lady whom the village kids called Mama 92 (because she was ninety-two years old; they renamed her every year), plugged her ears with her two bony hands and mumbled, sucking at her gums, *Aie aie, what a racket!*

We drank and ate late into the night. On the menu was leg of lamb, roast venison, potatoes in duck fat, thick slices of fresh sausage, garlic butter, cured sausage, smoked bacon, whole wheat bread, fresh walnuts, wild asparagus, and stuffed cabbage. As for alcohol, there was so much and so many kinds that I can't remember what we drank, much less in what order. We were drunk even before we'd eaten our fill. Sitting at the tables, out of the sun, beneath the cedar branches, we sang at the tops of our lungs, mouths full. The children laughed to see us reverting to childhood. We got carried away over nothing, invigorated by the joy of being together, all of us gifted at becoming emotional in no time at all. We took turns leaving to pee behind the farm, in copses of chamomile and lilac flowerbeds. In the silence interspersed with piercing moos, we could see the stony road dance, and the comfort of physically relieving ourselves added to our rapture.

Long after the sun had set, our minds calmed by the night, I remember sitting on a chair at a big deserted table. It was midnight, or maybe a little later. The air hadn't cooled yet. My head was spinning, my tongue stiff as a piece of cardboard in my dry mouth. I had eaten too much, drank too much, talked too much.

I had lost sight of you and the girls sometime late in the afternoon. I remember having spotted the children running in a pack from the courtyard to the granary and from the granary to the barn, never tiring. I had assumed they'd ended up falling asleep somewhere, our girls with them, piled one on top of the other in the hay like a litter of kittens lulled by the fresh air.

I didn't know where you were, but I wasn't worried. I imagined you were chatting under a lime tree or along the river, amid a cacophony of frogs.

In a drunken, vegetative daze, chin on my hands, I was contemplating what was left on the table: overflowing ashtrays, wine spilled on the paper tablecloth, half-eaten cream puffs. Many of the guests had gone home, but there were still enough of us to keep the party going. There were those talking quietly around the table, others, the oldest, dozing in their chairs, and then there were the ones standing up, smoking, while looking at the sky or else sluggishly twisting around on the dance floor, which was lit by a garland of paper lanterns. The newlyweds had disappeared, and their absence sparked a tender feeling of joy in us as we pictured them lying in the grass, brushing grasshoppers off their faces, intoxicated by kisses and the warm air. I'd learn later that, far from our romantic fantasies, our two lovebirds were in a deep sleep, drunk to the point of appearing dead, without having taken the time to undress or even take off their new shoes.

I raised my head toward the sky; it was pure, without complication. A gentle breeze rustled the cedar branches. The moment struck me as so delectable that I closed my eyes. I went inside myself with as much delight as if I was slipping into a warm bath. I reached a primitive state of serenity, rocked by the music and the whispers around the table.

It was at that exact moment that they materialized, two silhouettes glued together and coming toward us like some supernatural entity. The contrast between the depth of the night and the striking whiteness of their clothes no doubt reinforced the feeling of strangeness. Simon had told us that his future neighbors would be joining us, but when we didn't see them arrive at either the town hall ceremony or the reception, we had all thought they'd preferred not to come, and then we eventually forgot about them.

They approached hand in hand, in the thick night, without anyone seeming to notice them. The woman's heels clicked in the air. The slightly forced confidence with which they had appeared one moment earlier slowly disintegrated upon their contact with the warped cobblestones that covered the courtyard. Halfway across, they stopped, and I thought I detected some hesitation, but they resumed their walk toward us almost immediately.

Only then could I see them clearly. The woman was wearing a flowy dress that fell along her body so nicely that I could hardly, and only reluctantly, take my eyes off her. The man had on a white linen suit and a gray shirt. His black face melted perfectly into the night, giving the illusion that his body was headless. I looked around and realized that nobody had noticed them, or else, more likely, that the busy day had made everyone disinclined to standard courtesies, so I stood up and went over to welcome the new arrivals. I quickly introduced myself and apologized for Simon's absence. With a conspiratorial smile, encouraged by the reassuring darkness, I added, in a joking tone, that the young newlyweds surely had more important things to do. We shared a small forced laugh. *As it should be*, the man said to me, then turning to his wife, enveloping her in a gaze of immense tenderness, he added, *It is a very special day.* . . .

Moved by the thinly veiled reference to their own wedding, the woman nodded and then, discomfited by my presence, burst out laughing in joyful embarrassment.

I suggested they find a spot at the table and drink a glass of wine. The other guests, zoned out in their little bubbles, didn't pay any further attention to us. At least that's how it seemed. Of course it was nothing of the sort. I would quickly understand, given the many questions I was asked the next day, that their fake indifference hid very real interest.

I served them each a glass of wine, apologizing for

not toasting with them. *We're only staying a few minutes*, the man reassured me. He explained that given the late hour, they almost hadn't come, but having promised Simon they'd be present at his wedding, they'd felt duty-bound to honor the invitation.

His wife said she had family nearby, about ten miles away. *We come here a lot on vacation.* That was incidentally the reason they'd arrived so late; a family gathering had dragged on. I asked them where they had met Simon. *At the bar in the village, not even a week ago*, answered the man. *We came to show our land to our architect. We're going to build a house here.*

*Yes, I'm aware*, I responded. *Simon told me that you bought a plot not very far from my house, actually.*

*Oh, yeah?* asked the man, delighted.

*Yeah*, I answered. *The house fifty yards down.*

*The one with blue shutters, across the way?*

*Yes, that one!*

*Lovely to meet you, neighbor.*

That time, we shared a big laugh.

The conversation continued a while longer. Then, quite naturally, it fizzled out and silence settled in between us.

The man and the woman looked at each other and smiled, and their eyes said what their lips couldn't express.

I thought to myself that they must be a new couple, but in reality (I'd learn this later) they'd been married for fifteen years and had three children between seven and twelve years old. The comparison with my own relationship was inevitably painful. You and I didn't look at each other with that intensity anymore, despite the love we shared. I don't know why that observation made me a little sad. I quickly managed to convince myself that their show of tenderness didn't mean anything—that love could be modest, too, and that it wasn't measured by how strongly it was displayed. When they stood to say goodbye, making me promise to give Simon and the new bride a hug from them, I felt relieved. I watched them disappear into the night, speeding up as though they were worried about missing an appointment. By their quickening steps, I guessed they were in a hurry to be alone again. My tense body relaxed. Nothing remained but immense fatigue.

On the Monday after the wedding, I went to the Tennessee, the bar run by François. It was going on noon. The two village old-timers were at the counter, like they were every other day, snickering into their tanned hands and lapping up their noon Suze. On paper, their names are Lucien and Léon. But we called them Abbott and Costello because you never found one without the other, and because their favorite pastime was adding new jokes to their repertoire. On occasion, folks referred to them as Laurel and Hardy, too.

Lucien was fat and chatty; Léon was more subdued and looked like a beanpole. Some said that if one died, the other would follow. Former farmworkers, they'd known each other since their first steps and had only ever left the country to fight in the Aurès, in Algeria, in the same regiment. Despite their age, they never sat, preferring to wedge their bellies (as pronounced in the fat one as in the beanpole) against the edge of the bar, standing shoulder to shoulder. The two of them together didn't take up more room than one would.

Behind the bar, François always attentively listened to their latest jokes and smiled, often just to be polite and almost always out of indulgence, owing to their advanced age. He'd perfected his fake listening skills, thanks no doubt to the large, protruding ears that earned him the nickname Mickey, after the cartoon.

As soon as he noticed me on the doorstep, Lucien called out, *How's it going, Anna? All good, sweetheart?*

I waved hello to everyone. The two friends smiled widely, showing all their teeth; they hadn't lost a one. I ordered a coffee, and they each got another Suze.

*You know why they write "virgin wool" on sweaters?* Lucien asked me.

I answered that no, I didn't.

*Because sheep run faster than shepherds!*

We burst out laughing. François chuckled silently behind the counter.

The bar was empty at that hour of the day. A few flies overcome by the muggy air languished on the deserted tables. At low volume, for background noise, a Johnny Hallyday song was playing. François was an especially big fan and listened to him from morning to night. Lucien and Léon didn't like Johnny. Between themselves, they secretly called him Johnny-Loves-the-Payday.

We talked about Simon's wedding, which was all anyone was talking about. Of course, the whole village, or nearly, had been invited. Lucien said that it had been a great party and that the venison thigh had been tender. *I drank so much I almost couldn't find my way home! I got chewed out by my wife real good! Took me all of yesterday to sober up. You, too, am I right, Léon?* His friend snickered, dry fingers over his mouth, then gulped down what was left of the Suze. Without waiting, François served him a refill.

Not a soul was outside. The heat had forced everybody into seclusion. Lucien, looking through the tall glass door, said, *Hot summer this year, ain't it? Even the river's losing its water. Noticed it yesterday when I was walking, down a good third.*

In the distance we could hear the steel blade of a saw

wailing and cows mooing, half as loud as in winter; they suffered from the heat, too. The sound of bells from the neighboring village, carried by a burning wind, echoed at length. We decided that someone must have died; we figured someone old, always better than someone young. *Or worse, a child*, said François. Then the ringing abruptly stopped.

The smells of fried peppers, dry hay, sizzling onions, and pizza dough filled the street baking beneath the sun and drifted into the Tennessee, blending with the hints of aniseed, Suze, and martini that permeated its walls.

In one hour, bodies would slump under the village roofs, felled by sleep—the siesta—and minds enveloped in a clammy slumber would stop struggling.

Two tourists came in, a man and a woman. And it was as if the enchantment vanished, as if the glistening sweat on their foreheads pulled us back to the uncomfortable mugginess of everyday life. We recognized them as tourists by their extreme blondness and their inevitably sunburned skin. In broken French, they asked for the way to the Chemin des Oeillets. They were very cheerful, bowing exaggeratedly to apologize for the bother. François gave them directions; they bowed again, then left. Lucien turned toward Léon and tossed out, *Always something on the Fritz, eh!*

And off they went, laughing again. I laughed, too. I'd have liked to ignore the terrible joke, but I gave in, as I did every time, patronizingly perhaps, but also out of respect for their age. François snorted. It seemed like he was thinking, Getting old doesn't excuse everything, but what he actually murmured was *Come on, let's not pile on the blondies. They keep business going, after all. . . .*

This led to a discussion between Lucien and Léon.

*Did you notice that their socks went up to their knees? All you could see was their thighs!*

*Socks, in this weather!*

*Once I caught two of 'em copulating behind a bed of geraniums, asses bright red, I swear. What a gas!*

*Well, those are the Germans for you, or the Dutch, and maybe the Belgians, too.*

*Can you imagine? They walk all day long in the blistering heat—that's what they save up for.*

*And at night, they don't even sleep in a hotel, right? They prefer a tent. . . .*

*No accounting for tastes. . . .*

Then, Léon abruptly asked me, as though one thought

had prompted the next, *Who was that guy at Simon's, the one who came after the wedding was over?*

He didn't dare say the Black guy. Here, we laughed openly at Germans, because it was allowed—the war gave us that right. Same for the Dutch and the Belgians. We basically viewed them as an extension of the Germans. But we'd never had any Black people in Carmac.

I didn't have time to answer because a group of three young boys noisily walked in. They mumbled hello and headed to the back of the bar. We knew all of them; we'd grown up with their parents. They sat near the foosball table and ordered hard lemonades.

One of the boys asked another, *What the fuck were you doing at the chapel?*

We could hear their conversation perfectly. They were convinced that we couldn't, as though there were a soundproofed wall in the center of the bar separating our world from theirs, making us invisible and, most important, deaf in their eyes.

The other boy answered, talking a mile a minute, like he was afraid his friends wouldn't let him finish his story: *I was walking Mama 92's dog she can't get around no more since they put in her titanium knees she gives me twenty euros to take out her rat she says the chapel's good for the mutt 'cause he likes to visit his dead dog buddies there's plenty of 'em buried there he knows the place by heart but goddamn the fucking rat pisses everywhere and it freaks the fuck outta me but come on for twenty euros I ain't gonna say nothin' and get this when I brought her back her toilet bowl brush of a dog she kissed him right on the mouth "Come here baby come spoil your mama" it's seriously fucked up and get this the little furball shit stuck its tongue in 92's mouth the dog had just pissed and taken a crap and licked its own ass ugh and after that the old hag grabs my arm and doesn't let go she tells me her boring-ass stories about her titanium knees seriously dudes if I'd had a gun I'd have popped the two of them the old bag and her shitsack dog. . . .*

He shook his head, out of breath, like he'd just escaped some terrible accident. Then he joined the other two, who had moved to the foosball table.

As soon as the ball rebounded, Lucien, taking advantage of the noise produced by its dull roll, exclaimed, as if to himself, *It's true, we don't see too many brutes like that around here!*

I didn't immediately understand what he was referring to. Visibly, neither did François. He looked at me, then at Lucien. His wide-open eyes seemed to be taking over from his ears, which, big as they were, couldn't decode what the old man had said. Léon, who could figure out anything provided it came from his friend, responded immediately. *The last ones we saw were in the Aurès, right? You remember, the Senegalese shooters!*

*How could I not?! They were tearing you apart by the looks of it. . . .*

Then both men began to stare at the bottles behind the bar, consumed by the same wild terror. It was like their pupils were shrinking as the movie of their lives played in reverse, going so far back that their wrinkled faces slowly gave way to other, smooth faces baked by the Algerian sun on the steep slopes of a craggy mountain.

Their silence dug a breach into which the three young boys' conversation quite naturally slipped back. Back at their table, sipping their hard lemonades, they said every sentence in a monotone, as though none of them had any meaning, or the opposite, as though they all meant the same thing.

*Is it normal to have a dick that curves to the right?*

*Not normal. Kill yourself. It's over.*

*You jerk off too much.*

*For real?*

*Totally. When you jerk off too much, it creates microfractures in your dick.*

*For real?*

*I'm completely for real.*

*Stick it in a door and swivel your hips to the left, that should do it.*

*Fuck off, asshats! Watch me fucking destroy you at foosball!*

And with a roar of laughter, they got up and returned to their positions, exactly the same as before, to continue their game as if nothing had interrupted it.

Looking into Lucien's and Léon's eyes, you'd have thought that the lights had been abruptly turned back on. Nothing in particular seemed to have happened to have changed their mental state, but the terror in their eyes had ceded to a kind of suspicious curiosity. I picked up the conversation where we had left off. I told them that the unknown guest at Simon's wedding was our future neighbor; that his name was Bakary Langlois; that he was going to build a chalet at the entrance to the village, not far from my house; that he had three children and that he ran a company. When I said *ran a company*, I noted that a nervous twitch betrayed some confusion in the two old-timers. In their minds inhabited by Senegalese ghosts, a Black man couldn't be the head of a company. The Black man worked for the white man, not the reverse.

I told them about the plot where our future neighbor had decided to build his house. Land was precisely the thing that had occupied them their whole lives.

*Do you know the history of that plot?* Lucien asked me.

I answered that I didn't.

*Well, fifteen or so years ago, they were gonna build a big hotel, pool and everything, for the tourists. They brought in architects, contractors, workers, tons of folks. But it never got done. I dunno what happened really, it just never got done. Had to have been about money, am I right?*

Léon said that the mayor must be relieved to have sold it. *He didn't know what the hell to do with that land after that. . . .*

I added that construction on the chalet would start in a few weeks and that based on what Mr. Langlois had told me, they would move in as soon as possible.

Léon was visibly struggling to understand why people like them would deliberately choose to live in a village like ours. He asked me, mistrustfully, why they'd come here.

*I'm not sure. He told me he needed a little authenticity. That's what he said—authenticity.*

*Authenticity*, repeated Léon, like he was expecting me to explain what it meant. But I didn't say anything else.

François said, *Living in peace . . . now that's authenticity.*

Staring at his glass of Suze, Lucien muttered under his breath, *Well, we'd like to live in peace, too.*

No one seemed to have heard. Léon nodded, that was all.

Then we stopped talking.

The foosball rolled in one direction, then another, in a frantic rhythm. In the background, Johnny, always.

The two old men's telephones began ringing in their pants pockets a few seconds apart. They were expected for lunch.

*C'mon, our ladies have rung the Angelus. See ya tomorrow, François. Later, sweetheart!*

They walked out, shoulder to shoulder. As soon as they set foot on the burning asphalt, their two bodies separated, sagging beneath the direct sunlight, like the sky was crushing them with all its weight.

We watched them disappear, their hesitant steps scrunching on the gravel. I heard a final complaint.

*Goddamn heat! So this is the hill I choose to fry on!*

*And to think that then winter's so cold that we freeze our Algiers off!*

François gave me a sympathetic look, and before I could respond in kind, two conspiratorial cackles rang out beneath the sun's white rays, underscoring the silence.

*T*here's one thing I fail to understand, *Mr. Guillot*, said the judge, crossing his arms.

Your head was lowered, like someone walking into a strong wind.

*Would you be kind enough to sit up straight and look at us when you're being spoken to?* he asked in a calm voice. *Have the courage to face us.*

You sat up and your lips quivered.

*Thank you, Mr. Guillot.*

You managed to stammer out a *Sorry* that got lost in your throat, then you lifted your head, biting your lips.

Someone in the room coughed, an endless, dry cough that exasperated the judge. *Articulate, please, Mr.*

*Guillot. From the start we haven't understood a word you've said!*

You looked at him, more lost than ever. In your confusion, you finally let out a timid *Beg your pardon?* that disconcerted everyone, including me, who in sixteen years of communal living had never heard that expression come out of your mouth.

The judge opened his eyes wide and with a half-smile asked, *Are you mocking me?*

You shook your head no, and despite your best efforts, you teared up.

The judge took a short breath, then slowly formulated his question as though he was addressing a child or a stranger who didn't speak his language. *Mr. Guillot, why, after washing your hands in the frozen river, did you return to the house to steal objects belonging to members of the Langlois family?*

He pulled a sheet of paper from his file and read: *"Young Marion's cellphone, a half-empty bottle of perfume, four CDs, two DVDs, two children's books, a digital camera, a computer mouse, and a box of cigars."*

He looked up at you and said, *Something for everyone.* He clicked his tongue, then added, *You murdered, then you went back to help yourself. Do you have an explanation for me?*

Met with silence, he continued, *These are things that you could have bought for yourself. Your salary plus what your wife was getting for her parental leave allowed for some indulgences. So I'll ask my question again: Why did you steal these ordinary objects?*

You shook your head idiotically.

*Were you consumed by jealousy, desire, greed?* The judge went on: *Did you wish you had Mr. Langlois's nice cars?*

You answered yes, with a bizarre moan, that you thought they were nice, but that was it.

*And his chalet, did you want that, too?*

*Yes,* you answered flatly. *I mean yeah, everyone thought it was great, but . . .* Your throat constricted, preventing you from continuing.

At that, the judge said in an incredibly gentle voice, *I'm not interested in "everyone." We need to hear what you think, you, here in this courtroom.*

You shriveled up in your chair. All we could see were your shoulders.

*Please sit up, Mr. Guillot.*

I glimpsed a sort of damp terror in your eyes.

The judge swallowed, then said, *You had a serious accident a few years ago, isn't that right?*

You nodded.

He continued, *You were destined for a high-level athletic career, but an unfortunate fall squashed those hopes. That must have been very painful for you.*

You knew exactly where he was going. That's why you said nothing.

Undeterred, the judge continued, *You certainly must have fantasized about the wonderful life you could have had, didn't you? Did Mr. Langlois's success upset you? According to the experts, your jealousy of Mr. Langlois's life was all-consuming, to the point of making you forget what you already had. Wouldn't you agree, Mr. Guillot?*

You said nothing.

The judge shook his head and rubbed the back of his neck, closing his eyes. Then, leaning over his file: *I'll cite the expert once again. "To become as desirable as Mr. Langlois. That's what Constant Guillot yearned for with all his being. But when the object of his longing expanded to 'immaterial attributes,' meaning the Langloises' rock-solid marriage, the warmth of their home, the carefree-ness of their children, and so on, and he became aware that he could never attain such success, there was no other resort but the use of violence. He went so far as to hold Mr. Langlois responsible for his failures."*

The judge looked up at you. *It was you or him. You*

*chose yourself, Mr. Guillot. The insignificant objects that
you stole after wiping out an entire family were no doubt
more symbolic than functional. Possessions filled with
meaning, with a prestige to which you aspired, don't you
think?*

You didn't say a word.

The judge added, before he stopped talking, *What
matters is what you say—you, not what I read.*

Your lawyer hadn't said anything as you were being
questioned. He could have intervened to save you from
drowning, but he was outmatched.

The judge leaned back in his chair, furtively glancing at his watch, then said the trial was adjourned until
that afternoon. You shook your head, like you were trying to swat away a fly.


When the trial resumed, the prosecutor asked you if you
were racist.

You squinted, as if you were trying to see in bright
sunlight. All you could think to say was a long-drawn-
out *Wait . . .* , which everyone in the audience took for
an admission.

The question, visibly too direct, had completely

disconcerted you. The prosecutor looked at the jurors, delighting in the impact of your disastrous hesitation, then said, *You did realize that Mr. Langlois was Black, right?*

An outburst of laughter. And you laughed, too, sending your lawyer into a rage. He glared at you. You went pale and immediately shut your mouth.

*I'm glad to see that all this amuses you, Mr. Guillot,* said the prosecutor, smiling like a cat that had gotten the cream.

I didn't understand what was happening to you. You were acting like a dumb schoolboy caught up in something, with no awareness of the catastrophic repercussions that such a feckless attitude could bring about. Everything was compounding the negative image you were projecting: your puzzling behavior, your suicidal refusal to cooperate, the prosecutor's insistence on making you out to be a monster by distinguishing you from the rest of society. You were sinking miserably without even putting up a fight.

The prosecutor resumed: *Is it true that you called him the "big darkie"?*

You said nothing, chewing on the inside of your cheeks.

He continued, *Numerous accounts mention verbal and racial abuse: "the darkie," "the African upstart," and even "the ape swimming in cash." Is that right, Mr. Guillot?*

You reluctantly said that maybe, yes, once or twice, but that you didn't think it at all.

*What is it that you didn't think, Mr. Guillot, that Mr. Langlois was a "darkie" or that he was "an African upstart"?*

You shook your head, then angrily mumbled, *Okay, yeah, sometimes, between us, we'd say "the big darkie" . . . but it's . . . it's not an insult. . . . It's got nothing to do with racism, they're words, they're just words. . . .*

Your lawyer disappeared inside his robe. The prosecutor gave you a long stare, then said, *Mr. Guillot, at the risk of being repetitive, are you racist, yes or no?*

You looked at your lawyer, his face deformed by a bitter fake smile.

After a long silence you said, slightly breathless, *No, I'm not racist.*

*But you called him an "ape"!*

*I just said it to say it!*

*To say it?*

*Yes, because I was angry!*

*Elaborate, please.*

*I spoke without thinking.*

*Did his presence upset you?*

*No, but I couldn't stand to be scammed by someone not from this country. . . .*

The prosecutor opened his eyes wide. He finally had you. *Mr. Langlois was "from this country," as you put it! He was French, the same as you or me!*

*That's not what I meant at all! I'm not racist. You're twisting my words. It's not because of the color of his skin. He swindled us. He humiliated me. And it's like that doesn't matter!*

The prosecutor took a deep breath. *Okay, let's look at the situation another way, if you don't mind. Let's imagine that the person who moved in across from you one day had the same lifestyle as Mr. Langlois, had swindled you in the same way, but was white. Would you have acted in the same way?*

Your lawyer intervened, *Objection!*

The judge immediately overruled him and asked you to answer.

*This is ridiculous*, you said. *Skin color has nothing to do with it! He cheated us, remember!*

The prosecutor's regrettably sensationalist question didn't merit a response. But the judge had decided otherwise. Your lawyer was shooting daggers at you. The prosecutor continued, *That's clearly an obsession of yours! Does that justify killing him and his entire family? How much did he swindle you out of? Eight thousand euros? Eight thousand euros! You killed five people for eight thousand euros! Not much at all!*

You touched your neck, then your lips, like you were going to throw up. You said, *Yes, that's true, but in the moment, I didn't think about that. It was my parents' money, all their savings, what was I going to tell them? Eight thousand euros is still a lot of money. . . .*

The prosecutor interrupted you immediately, appalled at how hollow your words sounded. *And Mr. Langlois's children? Did they swindle you, too? What about their mother? What did that poor woman do to you to merit being riddled with bullets? There's no evidence that she was aware of her husband's scams. None. Do you really believe that their deaths were worth eight thousand euros? One thousand six hundred euros per person, Mr. Guillot. You don't think that's a measly sum in relation to the gravity of your actions?*

Before sitting back down, he spat out, *We live in a sick world!* Then he indicated to the judge that he had nothing more to add.

The judge asked you if you had anything to say. You

answered that your mind was all muddled, that you were sick of people twisting your words, and that from now on, you'd prefer to keep quiet.

The judge, strangely calm, leafed through his file. Evening fell. He adjourned the trial.

knew the instant I saw you running down that track that we would have a future together.

The stadium that drew so many athletes of all different levels was also, thanks to its proximity to the high school, the place where everyone would gather after classes ended for the day. A few school friends and I used to sit on the bleachers and watch the athletes in motion as we chatted and smoked, like we were watching the sea from up on a cliff. Sometimes we'd even share a lukewarm beer that we drank straight from the bottle, passing it from person to person.

That day, you'd been training for over an hour and I hadn't been able to take my eyes off you. It was the first time I'd ever seen you. Your sport, pole-vaulting, was pretty rare around here, and it fascinated me. Each time you launched yourself down the track, it seemed as if you were running for your life, as if it was your last jump. After every attempt, you would turn toward your coach. He talked, you listened. Hanging on to his every word, you would silently agree with a simple nod or quick slide of your hand through your hair. There was a fierce determination about you, an unwavering obstinacy that captivated me on the spot. It was as though nothing could distract you from your objective. Everything in you, body and mind, seemed to be focused on a single goal: jump as high as possible.

When I asked my friends if any of them knew you, they all told me no. I later learned that you had just moved to the area with your parents and that both they and your coaches expected a lot from you, and that given your remarkable talent, it was unimaginable that you wouldn't become a champion. A destiny for which your parents were willing to sacrifice their money and your coaches their time. After winning the local championship, you took first place at regionals; your exceptional scores were leading you straight to qualifying for France's national team.

Every evening, I would look out for a glance, a small sign, but nothing. To my great despair, you stayed focused, gripping your pole as if it was an extension of you. No doubt nothing would have happened between us if I hadn't benefited from a little nudge from my crew, who, neither stupid nor blind, had clearly noticed that my presence at our stadium meetups wasn't solely motivated by my friendship with them but also, and especially, by how happy it made me to watch you. Of course, at first, I denied any attraction, but my unvarying objections ultimately worked against me. My friends' reaction was amused incredulity; I was forced to admit that yes, oh, yeah, I liked you a lot.

One night, you walked into the pizza place where we were all gathered and joined our group. To my great surprise, everyone seemed to know you. They had you sit across from me, in the middle of the table, so that everyone could watch us. I couldn't bring myself to look in your direction even once. The evening had been arranged with the sole goal of connecting us, and everything that was said, all the questions asked of you, were meant to give me information. Despite their good intentions, my friends had placed me in a terribly awkward situation. But you played along, not without a hint of mischief. Despite my discomfort, I didn't miss a word you said. No point in adding that nothing happened that evening, and that the next day, after biting my nails all night long, I called my friends one by one to tell them how much I hated them. I was convinced that their interference had ruined everything and, most important, that I would never recover from the embarrassment.

That very afternoon I received a message on my cellphone in which you invited me to the movies the following weekend. One year later, you asked me to marry you, and of course I said yes.

Your parents didn't look too favorably on our relationship, convinced that I was distracting you from your bright future. As a young man, your father had also attracted attention for his athletic talents, in soccer, but sadly never got a chance to play professionally because of his increasingly lackluster performance on the field. That outcome hadn't been easy for him to accept, but the second he met your mother, he turned the page without bitterness, immersing himself in a mechanical studies program and becoming an excellent mechanic. His life as a great athlete seemed like a distant dream, and nothing since had ever made him think back to that time. A first child was born; a second followed; then you arrived, the youngest of an all-male trio. Unlike your brothers, during your school years you demonstrated rare athletic abilities to which your parents were quickly alerted.

Boosted by this new opportunity that life was offering him through you, your father felt the rekindling of an inner fire that he had thought long extinguished. Miraculously reinvigorated, he decided that you wouldn't miss out on something he hadn't been able to see through himself. To that end, he would commit his will, his time, and his money. That's why when I showed up it was quickly made clear to me through constant hints that it would be criminal to divert you from your goals. I was forced to carry the weight of your failure before you had even failed. The unfairness with which I was treated was doubly painful since you never objected in the slightest to the unspoken threats your parents allowed to linger in the air between one silence and the next.

Whenever we found ourselves alone again and I'd ask you why you hadn't said anything, you would invariably respond that I shouldn't take your parents seriously, that you couldn't care less what they thought, and that it was pointless to start a fight over nothing. The *nothing* that you wielded every time I expressed my bafflement wounded me; it was a frightening forewarning that my interloper presence would change absolutely nothing about the life you had led with your parents up till then and that whatever might happen, you would be on their side unconditionally. I even found myself wondering whether your parents' disapproval of me actually suited you. Over time, I started to doubt your sincerity, too, and your love. But in spite of my grim prognosis, you asked me to marry you. Seeing my astonishment, you burst into such honest, transparent laughter that it instantly swept away all my uncertainty.

When our plans to wed were announced, your parents were silent and stern. As usual, you shrugged and said you didn't care what they might think. That time, unlike in the past when those hurtful words had caused me such pain, I felt pride in hearing you say them in my favor.

It was April; we were meant to marry in October. You said that you loved me; that's what you would whisper to me at night, after making love. *I love you so so much*, you would say. I'd respond, *Me, too*, head buried in your armpit, in the musky smell of your soft hairs that tickled my nostrils.

One day, during a practice jump, your pole bent due to a technical error—your shoulders were too far back—and pitched you violently across the track. You fell from the height it had propelled you to, which is to say nearly four yards in the air.

Even before the bones in your pelvis shattered from

the force of the impact, you knew that it was over and your dreams of glory were destroyed for good.

The surgeon who saw us at the hospital explained that the state of your pelvis was like that of a broken vase and that your femur was fractured, too, and as a result, they would have to insert an artificial one with pins. Crazed with rage and pain, your father kept muttering, seemingly to himself, *What the hell happened? What the hell happened with that goddamn pole?!*

But you knew that these accidents occurred, that a simple miscalculation could cause what you pole-vaulters called a throwback. It was one of the worst possible scenarios, and unfortunately you hadn't been spared.

Hands over her mouth, your mother choked back sobs. She cast me a beseeching look, as though I held the power to go back in time and erase the absurdities that the old surgeon was reeling off. I approached her and, without thinking, took her in my arms.

Like a child waiting for nothing more than a warm hug to give into her pain, she violently burst into tears. I couldn't tell if the cause of her pain was the tragic accident that had befallen you or the fierce animosity she'd always shown me and now regretted.

Your father was watching from a distance, somewhat

taken aback by his wife's reaction. But from deep within his tremendous grief, he looked at me like he was seeing me for the first time. And miraculously, he smiled.

After eight months of hospitalization and eight months of intensive rehabilitation, you walked again. Before that, you had to endure numerous complications related to the severity of your fractures. Your bladder, damaged in the fall, had to be stitched up on two occasions, and a paralysis of your sciatic nerve led to a permanent limp. You became mute and taciturn. At the hospital, all that interested you was the television screen you stared at from morning till night and, judging from the deepening circles under your eyes, well into the early hours. The only thing you refused to watch was sports. If you accidentally landed on anything related, you would immediately change the channel and the melancholy clouding your gaze abruptly transformed into silent fury. You never watched a single track-and-field competition again. For many months, you lost interest in sports entirely.

You ate very little. You would snack on the salted nuts that I bought at the hospital minimart, at your request. Convinced that your lack of appetite was related to the disgusting food being served to you, your mother would bring you home-cooked meals in still-warm

Tupperware. You didn't touch them. You would thank her with a frozen smile, then tiredly push away everything she presented. Your mother would beg softly, patting your arm, *Try it, sweetheart. Come on, baby boy.* She'd begun using certain words for the first time since you were a child: *sweetheart, baby boy, darling.* But this just annoyed you, sending you into a dull rage.

Your father would stay standing in a corner of the room, completely still, staring at you with a worried look. You weren't eating, but he was the one wasting away, as if through symbiotic attachment, he had chosen to spare you one more misfortune by shrinking in your stead. You never talked about what you were going through; you acted as if nothing affected you. But if any mention was made of the old days, you'd stiffen and with a few biting sentences firmly let us know that you had zero interest in your former life.

On top of your depression, your body was prone to inexplicable drops in temperature. You were cold constantly. In your hands, your feet, everywhere. And long after you were discharged, at the height of summer, you continued to shiver. You didn't understand what was happening to you and attributed the strange phenomenon to the lack of exercise. I thought that you were stuck in some kind of traumatic winter.

When you left the hospital, we moved into a small furnished apartment that belonged to my parents. They had always rented it out, but since they'd paid off the mortgage some time before, they had no objections to us moving in until, as they put it, we could *stand on our own two feet*. I found the expression a little insensitive when directed at someone who could barely stand. But I comforted myself by thinking that, given your distractedness since the accident, you hadn't noticed.

Despite your sadness, which left a permanent look of pain on your face, you gradually began to feed yourself again. You didn't know how you were meant to imagine your future yet—you hadn't even thought about it, actually. In any case, I expected nothing from you. I was only concerned with the improvement of your overall condition and supporting you as best I could.

That fall, I began a nursing program, something we'd discussed often before your accident; you'd seemed proud to be marrying a nurse. For as long as I can remember, I had always hoped to become one, like my mother. Her whole life, she had dedicated herself to the patients she used to call *my poor hurt dearies* with a gentle smile. She was deeply, movingly, attached to them; when one of them died, she took the loss as a personal failure.

When I'd come home at night, we would talk about any number of things, but I never asked you how you had spent your day. I knew that you'd done nothing and that your mind was filled with sorrow and memories. One night, you told me we deserved better.

*Better than what?* I asked.

You clumsily swept one arm around the apartment, then dropped it to your injured hip. You were crying noiselessly.

Your father had a hard time moving past the accident. In his mind, it was all a terrible curse. How was it possible for history to repeat itself? First him, then you. Two lives devastated, two destinies crushed, *some fucking life!*

Your mother spent her time reasoning with him, *He's alive, that's what matters!*

But nothing worked. Your father railed, he cursed God. *That son of a bitch ruined my son's life!*

He wasn't religious, never had been, but as strange as it might sound, your terrible fall had awakened his awareness of a divine presence. To him—and this was new— human will was subject to God's wickedness. Your tragic fate offered undeniable proof of the underhanded doings of a *fucking God* about whom he had never concerned himself before then. Someone had to be blamed.

His anger, which was merely the manifestation of his immense pain, upset you. At first, you acted like you always did: You didn't pay it any attention, convinced that his rage would subside in time. But though we expected otherwise, time only intensified his feelings. The exasperated powerlessness he expressed every time he saw you fueled your sense of inconsolable loss—of the person you had been and who you would never be again.

One night, a conversation degenerated into a fight. In exasperation, you told him that you couldn't stand his fatalistic attitude anymore, and that his anger, for all that it was legitimate, wasn't helping you move forward. You added that you were sick of his complaining and that you didn't understand why the situation affected him that much since, after all, he wasn't the one whose hip had shattered into little pieces or who was suffering from unbearable pain on a daily basis.

Your father looked at you as if he was seeing you for the first time or as if he was waking up from a long coma. He didn't object to any of your many reproaches; in fact, just the opposite—he seemed to welcome them as electrifying revelations.

Your mother was trembling on a little stool in the weak light of a lamp.

Your father didn't say a word and with a shaky head

motion invited his wife to follow him. We didn't see them for nearly three months. Your mother continued to call you when your father was out, to inform us of the radical change your last confrontation had brought about. He didn't talk about it at all anymore: *Not a word about your accident!* You felt the distance was necessary, convinced that you and he would reconcile one day when things had gone back to how they should be.

The estrangement proved beneficial. You began to look ahead again and consider a career change. But you had never pictured your life without sports, which made reframing your future more complicated than you had imagined. We would talk about it for entire evenings, and though you brought up various options, it was near impossible for you to picture anything other than athletics— that thing you had been intrinsically made for.

In the end, the solution came from elsewhere. You had stayed in close touch with your coach, who would stop by often to check on your health.

One day he told you that the regional handball team had lost its coach and they were looking to recruit a new one. At first, you dismissed the information with a sad laugh. *I've never touched a single handball, and anyway, sports are dead to me. I'm over it.*

The coach made a strategic retreat, knowing perfectly

well that he would wear you down; then, after a few days had gone by, he tried again. He came equipped with a rock-solid argument to counter every single one of your doubts, fiercely determined to convince you and overcome your legendary stubbornness.

*But,* you said, *how do you expect me to teach handball? I don't know the rules!*

*You don't need to have gone to Saint-Cyr,* responded the coach. *I'll teach you. All in all, there's only a dozen rules!*

*Plus I know nothing about coaching!*

*Same, I'll teach you.*

*But I'm still limping. It's hard for me to stand for more than an hour.*

*That'll pass with time, and anyway, you can train a team with your ass in a chair. And just so you don't waste any more breath, let me add that I'll come pick you up on nights when there's practice, until you can get behind the wheel again.*

He had an answer for everything.

*You really think I could?* you asked me that night, under the covers.

I answered, *Yeah, why not,* trying not to betray my worry. Ideally, I think I'd have rather you did something else. I was afraid that returning to the pursuit that had always given meaning to your life would foster eternal regrets and, worse, reawaken your immense grief for what you'd lost. How could you forget what you might have become if you were reminded of it every day?

You eventually gave in, and, against all odds, I witnessed an incredible rebirth. It was like the job had been created for you. You applied yourself with the fanatical determination I knew so well and that I had feared I would never see return. The melancholy that had clung to you until then disappeared as suddenly as it had appeared.

And as if one good thing wasn't enough, one day your father rang our doorbell. He fell into your arms before even crossing the threshold and cried for a long time. From the way you were holding him, one would have thought that you had become the father and he the child. I didn't dare disturb you at first; then, sensing the embrace loosening, I invited your father inside for coffee. In the kitchen, we drank our coffee without saying a word. We were like shipwreck survivors after a storm. Your father kept smiling, his eyes fixed on you. You were stirring your coffee with one hand and rubbing my arm with the other. We could hear the rain falling through the slightly open window and the whirring of the refrigerator. The smell of wet grass emanated from the ground. We felt enveloped by euphoria; it was as if everything had been designed to honor this fresh start. When you told your father that you had been offered a coaching position and that you had accepted it, his eyes lit up and new tears fell onto his cheeks. Between two convulsions, he managed to say, *When I tell your mother . . .*

Later, your mother told us that he had spent the night crying, and that the next day he was once again the man he had stopped being the day of your accident.

I continued my nursing studies until the end of my second year and then I gave up. My average, or rather mediocre, grades forced me to. I had to face facts—I wasn't made for this career path. In reality, I didn't have any healing talent. I had chosen to become a nurse because my mother had been one, but I soon realized that you can only do the job if deep in your gut you have an irrepressible need to fix other people. That wasn't me.

After that, I switched to a program in childcare. I spent two years working in the hospital nursery, then I got pregnant with our first child. When she was born, we bought our house and, wanting to raise my daughter myself, I took a parental leave of three years. Our second daughter arrived at the end of those three years, so quite naturally I took a second leave.

As the years went by, your condition improved,

so much so that you gradually went back to playing sports. Of course you no longer had the physique of a world champion, but you were still a talented athlete and your limp, less and less limiting, didn't stop you from playing well. The pain returned regularly, but you had learned to control it. Three times a week, you got in your car and drove the thirty-five miles that separated you from your place of work.

To look at you, it must have seemed as if you hadn't changed. You had gone back to being the man I'd known and there didn't appear to be any major differences in your personality. At least that's how it might have looked to someone who had just run into you. But I shared your life and knew you better than anyone. I could see clearly enough that something inside you had broken. Something that you had eventually put back together but whose delicate equilibrium risked giving way at any moment. Sometimes, for no particular reason, there'd be a stifled surge of rage in you, which I could detect from a gesture of impatience, or a faint sob in your voice, or a bitter laugh.

In those moments, it was as though you were an unpredictable volcano—a simple tremor was enough to make you explode. I remember thinking that you would find peace over time. And we kept moving forward.

We never talked about our aborted wedding. For that matter, we never got married. Sometimes I would have odd dreams in which we did. In those dreams, our clothes sparkled, and we smiled at people whose faces I didn't recognize. When you slid the ring on my finger, I looked up at your smile and noticed, in stupefaction, that you were missing every other tooth.

T he first snow fell heavy in the middle of November. The sky, black in spots, so low you could have punched it back with your fist, promised no improvement. At night, the valley wrapped itself in a premature silence. In the morning, behind the thick mist, not a single jackrabbit was left bounding down the snowy paths. In the village, hens deserted farmyards and hurried to warm themselves against the cows' boiling flanks.

On November 13, sitting in front of the television, we watched the terrible images of the terrorist attacks in Paris and Saint-Denis in horror. At first, we talked about them all the time—at home, at the grocery store, at the Tennessee, with everyone and everywhere. And then after a week we didn't have anything else to say. Silence, like the inert snow, gradually settled back in.

The chalet construction, which had begun a few months earlier, had to be interrupted. The early frost didn't necessarily foretell a long and difficult winter. In Carmac, it was impossible to predict the seasons because fickle nature would regularly contradict our forecasts. And that's exactly what happened. The snow melted in early January, and as the air warmed, birds once again took up residence in the trees' black branches. We heard them early in the morning as they jabbed at the bark, hopping on their thin legs.

Construction on the Langlois chalet resumed. We had glimpsed the couple on a few occasions, when they came to see how it was coming along, alone or with their three children. Sylvia was wearing a long wool coat and Bakary a parka with a fur collar and a Russian winter cap whose considerable volume made me smile. The children consistently refused to get out of the car, too busy hammering on their video games. They preferred to purr in the warmth of the back seat rather than confront the cold unnecessarily.

By early spring, the construction was complete. The chalet was the most impressive in the whole region; its appearance prompted both fear and admiration. Curiosity aroused, Abbott and Costello had changed the usual route of their daily stroll to stop in front of the chalet every morning. At their approach, I would open my kitchen window, taking in the air, and observe them. I'd hear them discussing the imposing house, both dumbfounded and dubious. Then they'd stare at it under the timid sun, the way you stare at something you're seeing for the first time. Hands in their pants' pockets, they would shrug their shoulders without saying a word.

One morning as I was walking out to meet them, Abbott yelled, *Hey, sweetheart, that house is gonna end up blocking your sun!*

I forced myself to laugh. We all paused for a moment to stare at the two-story chalet, lifting our heads to admire the thick roof frame in which it was still possible to make out fresh grooves with the naked eye.

*It's good work*, the two men agreed. *It's oak or chestnut. That kinda wood lasts forever. Costs a lot, but it's indestructible.*

The Langloises moved in at the end of June. We saw them arrive one clear and sunny morning in their enormous black car, followed by three moving trucks.

*Damn, a Hummer. That car's worth seventy grand!*

you said from behind our kitchen window as you pulled back the sheer curtains. It wasn't the only car they owned, we'd later realize.

The first week, I went over to welcome them. They greeted me warmly in return, but I sensed from their rushed movements that they preferred not to be bothered during the move. I had kindly offered my help, which they refused straightaway, claiming they didn't want to take advantage of me. But they still offered me coffee, which we drank quickly on their terrace overlooking the valley. The stunning view stretched on seemingly endlessly. We could see the black pinewood, the treetops jostled by the wind. The murmur of the river flowing through the valley blended with the sloshing coming from the old wash house. I'd known this place forever, but I felt like I was discovering it for the first time. The terrace was like a gigantic bird perch perfumed with the smell of pine resin carried aloft by the breeze; it made you want to soar into the sky.

In late August, the Langloises sent out invitations to a bunch of us. We got the cards in our mailboxes, which surprised and intrigued us. We weren't used to such social niceties; we didn't know what to think. In the village, people hardly ever invited one another over for dinner, and when they did it was usually for a special occasion, like a wedding or a baptism. The rest of the time, you'd drop by someone's house for coffee or drinks, but it wouldn't go beyond that.

At the Tennessee, François's bar, we were all wondering what the dinner party would be like. We asked around to find out who intended to accept the invitation and who would turn it down. We speculated as to whether there would be a buffet or a real meal. We were afraid we wouldn't know what to say to our new neighbors or that we would get bored, and we comforted ourselves with the thought that we'd be together. We made predictions about what kinds of drinks they'd offer. The oldest among us hoped there'd be Ricard; the youngest, beer; and the children, soda.

A good thirty of us ended up going. By chance, thanks to an Indian summer that year, the mild air allowed us to eat outside. The party took place on the terrace and, as was to be expected, everyone was dumbstruck by the incredible view.

Round tables and garden chairs had been set up everywhere. A multicolored string of lights stretched along the railing and tall outdoor lamps were standing guard in all four corners of the terrace. The warm wind, trapped in narrow lanes, rose weakly, lifting the tablecloths.

An impressive buffet was awaiting us on a long table. There were shrimp brochettes, potato pancakes, savory cakes (tomato, pesto), fish fritters, tuna tartare, thin melon slices, various kinds of salad, and cheese (Brie, Roquefort, Comté) presented under glass domes and served with walnuts and mesclun; chicken nuggets and macaroni and cheese for the children; and for dessert molten chocolate cake, tarte tatin with grilled-almond cream, and chocolate muffins. We drank wine (red and white), beer for those who preferred it, Ricard as an aperitif, port, white martini, soda, mineral water (flat and sparkling), and pear liqueur. A feast that left us all at a loss for words.

At first, none of us dared to approach the table. We kept our distance, shuffling around, hands behind our backs. We didn't know if we could serve ourselves or if we should wait for someone to offer. Thankfully, Sylvia invited us to come around the table, which we did, still unable to completely relax. Inside, the chalet was tastefully decorated. The high-quality furniture and rugs betrayed a certain affluence. Sylvia and Bakary went from one group to the next, friendly and smiling. Led by their children, our daughters ran through the house, going up and down the stairs, laughing, shouting, without being chastised once by either of our hosts.

Later that evening, a group formed around Bakary. Someone asked him what kind of work he did. He rushed to answer, as though he'd been waiting for that question ever since the evening began.

*My wife and I sell dreams. We created a travel agency different from the rest. A dream factory. We suggest trips to unusual places, like Mexico's Copper Canyon Railroad, for example. Do you know it? It's amazing! There's also Lapland on horseback, or immersion with the cowboys of the Outback, or a visit to Japan and its hot baths alongside the snow macaques. Our last idea was a trip around the world in forty days! It didn't exist before—it was my wife who thought of it. And soon we're going to offer a night under the stars on the roof of a Dubai skyscraper. It's looking good, people love it! Or else you can live like Robinson Crusoe on the islands of Vanuatu. And that's not all, we've got tons more ideas!*

Bakary took incredible pleasure from telling us about his work and his plans. I remember thinking that those trips had to be expensive and not at all accessible to people like us. Someone else asked him why they had chosen to make our village their home. Once again, his face lit up.

*My wife has family nearby. She's been coming here on vacation since she was little. She'd been dreaming of settling down here. Life is calmer in Carmac than in the city. We're a one-hour drive from our work, but we're willing to make the sacrifice!*

Bakary liked to talk. And for that matter every part of him talked: his eyes, his hands, his body. It was as if we were giving him the energy, by watching him, that fed his words. Unless it was the opposite. His wife was watching him from a distance, a glass of wine in her hand, with a strange, frozen smile.

You spent the evening with your eyes glued on him. He seemed to have some kind of hold over you. You didn't approach him that night. You couldn't. Later, I would catch you on our stoop contemplating the chalet, several nights in a row. It was as though your fascination was keeping you there, out of your control. At the kitchen window, I would part the curtains slightly to watch you. You would stand still, back straight, head raised toward the lit-up windows of the Langlois house, or else sit on the stone steps; some days the pain in your hips was more acute than others. Your mouth spat out white steam. Around you, night would fall little by little.

Bakary Langlois felt at home no matter where he was, with an ease that I found endlessly fascinating. His ability to melt into places and hearts stemmed no doubt from the defining event of his life: his adoption. His biological parents, living in extreme poverty in Gabon, had hoped to be able to provide for their large family (seven children), but devotion wasn't enough; impoverishment prevailed in the end. With heavy hearts, they decided to put their youngest child—four-year-old Bakary—up for adoption to give him a way out.

Bakary was adopted by a childless Parisian couple, intellectuals who had tried everything to conceive, in vain, as they approached their forties. They were frequent travelers, and Gabon was a country they knew very well, having visited it several times. That's why, when the time came, they returned and began the process of adopting a child there.

That's what Bakary told us one day when we ran into him in front of the chalet and he invited us to come have a drink on the terrace.

*My adoptive father was a newspaper journalist,* he said. *There were always people in our house. They came from all around the world. Sometimes there'd be more than fifteen of us sleeping in the apartment. We would put mattresses on the floor and we'd be good to go. My mother was a philosophy professor at the Sorbonne. Her thing was poker games with her colleagues and students. They would play all night long in the kitchen, smoking, eating chips. My mother hated losing; she would yell at everyone, a real battle-ax. . . . She died a few years ago. My father's still around, not really happy, but not unhappy, either. He does his best. . . .*

Bakary stopped short. He looked into the distance, above the pine trees, then turned to us and asked, *Does it hit you, too?*

Not understanding what he was talking about, we stared at him, waiting for clarification.

*Nostalgia*, he said. *Do you find yourselves feeling nostalgic, too?*

We said yes, of course, that we all do.

Bakary had never tried to find his biological parents. In his teens, his adoptive parents suggested a trip to Gabon, to the exact place where he had been adopted, to look for them. Bakary refused. He told us he had no memories of his biological parents and had never felt the need to know where he came from. He had been adopted and had accepted it completely. That was the story of his life; he didn't want any other.

It had been more than a month since Bakary and his family had moved in, and his pull over you hadn't diminished. But as we listened to him that day, I felt you relax. When you and I discussed the conversation that evening, I noticed that his sincerity had, in a way, rebalanced how you thought of him, and that your enthrallment had given way to respect.

Starting the next day your relationship took on a new cast. With as much spontaneity as he had shown, you opened up and told him about the tragic event that had upended your life. And since sharing misfortune often brings people together, the simple fact of you having confided in each other created an instant bond.

He started inviting you over on the weekends to hit a few baseballs in his massive garden. He'd belonged to a league for a while, but, as he said in a matter-of-fact way that left no room for regret, he was too old to be playing competitively. Because of your pelvis, you were happy just to catch the balls, which suited him perfectly; he swore that in any case his thing was hitting. When it rained, you and he would watch action movies on his gigantic television, or have a drink in his living room, beside the fireplace where a wood fire was burning. Bakary would invariably offer you a cigar, which you'd gently refuse, or a glass of wine, a nice vintage, that he would hand you, eyes shining, all smiles, adding that it wasn't exactly a wine from the mom-and-pop's, *you know what I mean?!*

The dining room, which was separated from the living room by an alcove, housed a library with bookshelves that covered three of its four walls. In the Langlois home, they inhaled the smell of paper as they ate. The impressive size of the library intimidated you—you'd never been a big reader—and when one day you finally dared to ask Bakary if he'd read all of the books, he burst out laughing, responding that he didn't see any point in having them in one's house just to watch them collect dust.

Bakary was more educated than all of the residents of the valley combined and yet nothing in his attitude revealed that aspect of his personality. He never acted like a know-it-all and, more surprising still, he could adapt to everyone, regardless of their schooling or social background. You couldn't decide if that was a positive character trait or a negative one.

Once, he suggested taking you for a drive in his massive black car. You came home pale that night.

*I've never seen anyone drive that fast,* you told me. *He was going over one hundred on the back roads!*

Bakary loved speed—it exhilarated and electrified him. He was particularly fond of narrow turns. You described how during the drive, approaching one of those turns, he let out whoops of delight that left you with a feeling of unease once the silence had returned.

On top of the Hummer (which I found ugly and flashy), Bakary and Sylvia had two other brand-new cars, a Mercedes and an Audi, which they alternated between depending on their outings and meetings. Bakary claimed that the Audi was perfect for meetings with his clients, that it impressed and reassured them, and established his credibility. The Mercedes, which Sylvia used fairly often, was, according to her, the ideal car for long drives or going to the movies or a restaurant.

Bakary had two fairly spacious garages built for the three cars, but most of the time his Hummer was parked in front of the house, like a guard dog of steel. He wasn't too meticulous about his vehicles but made it a point of honor to keep their hubcaps clean and shiny. He cleaned them almost every day with a dry rag and on the weekend with soap and water. That compulsion left you perplexed, especially since he didn't seem interested in the rest of the bodywork.

In reality, the more time you spent with him, the more inscrutable he became. He was both a thing and its opposite. It was as if multiple planets had violently collided, but instead of exploding, they fused together.

*That guy*, you would say, *is the opposite of the big bang!*

That was why you started calling him that, though only around me. At night, you would say, *You know what Big Bang did?* Or, *You know what Big Bang said?*

And then eventually you dropped the *Bang* and only kept the *Big.* You felt like *Big* went well with his build. And Bakary was in fact big and tall. Actually, everything about him was big, including his appetite for life. He was the kind of guy who would welcome everyone, man or woman, with a hearty pat on the back, radiating an unusual vitality. He was more alive than any of us had ever been, and all of us were grateful for his big beaming smile. Everyone here adopted him in the end. I wouldn't have been surprised to learn that everywhere he went, he was greeted with the same warm welcome.

*D*id you enter the Langlois family's house with the firm intention of killing them?

It was a critical question. The entire trial was riding on determining whether, yes or no, you had gone to the Langlois home with *the firm intention of killing them*. Was it a fleeting moment of madness or a premeditated act? Your lawyers were sticking to the first version, doing everything to provide evidence for it. They deemed it essential to rule out premeditation, which was considered an aggravating factor. If the jurors decided your actions had been premeditated, you risked life in prison.

To the question *Did you have the intention of killing the Langlois family?* you responded no. Your lawyer added that you hadn't brought a weapon into the house, which was clear proof of what you were claiming.

The prosecutor said that you had nonetheless returned to your garage to get your rifle after murdering the children and that you had waited for the parents to come home from work, crouching for more than half an hour behind the door of their chalet with the sole goal of taking them out.

*If that's not premeditation, then what is?!*

You responded that if you had wanted to kill them, you would have gotten the weapon right away.

*I just wanted to talk to Mr. Langlois. I was in a rage. He refused to give me back my money, I hadn't slept in three whole days. I wanted to talk to him, that's all. It's true, I swear. I just wanted him to give me back my money.*

You were asked: *Why did you own a rifle? Do you hunt?*

*No, it's my father's rifle. My mother asked me to keep it at my house because she felt that my father was too old to be hunting . . . She was scared there'd be an accident.*

You were asked what had gone through your mind to compel you to murder five people. The question threw you off. You said, *I don't really know how to explain it. . . .*

The judge encouraged you to express yourself.

*Mr. Guillot, it's important for you that you help us understand what happened.*

You nodded yes, twice. The judge smiled, then began.

*What time was it when you decided to go over to the Langlois home?*

*Going on six p.m.*

*Be specific, please.*

*Between five forty-five and six, something like that. I'm sorry. I don't remember.*

*Did your wife see you leave?*

*No, she was grocery shopping with the kids.*

*Where?*

*The supermarket at the shopping center. Right off the highway.*

*How far is it from your home?*

*About twenty miles.*

*Did she know you intended to pay a visit to Mr. Langlois to ask him for your money back?*

*Yes. I had been going there every night for a week.*

*What did she think of that?*

*She was sick of it.*

*But that night, you were more agitated than usual?*

*I had been yelling at the girls all day long. I wasn't sleeping anymore. It was starting to make me crazy.*

*And it didn't worry your wife when you told her that
you were planning to go to the Langloises'?*

*She didn't say anything.*

*Did she know that you were keeping your father's
rifle in the garage?*

*She knew.*

*What time did she leave to go grocery shopping?*

*She left at five o'clock.*

*Five o'clock exactly?*

*Yes.*

*You can give me the precise time for your wife but
not for you?*

*She's obsessed with schedules. It's like that for every-
thing: meals, the kids' bath time, errands. Grocery shopping
is always Monday at five o'clock.*

*And what time does she get back from the super-
market?*

*Seven thirty.*

*And that's always exactly the same, too?*

*Yes.*

*And always with the children?*

*After the groceries, she takes them on the merry-go-
round. There's one on the second floor of the shopping
center.*

*That gives you some time.*

*What do you mean?*

*The time to do what you wanted without being disturbed.*

*I didn't plan to kill them.*

*Leave it to us to decide.*

*I'm not a liar.*

*Mr. Guillot, please limit yourself to answering the questions.*

*Okay, understood.*

*Good. Did you know that the Langlois children were alone?*

*No. Usually the parents were there at that hour. Occasionally they'd get home later, but not often.*

*And yet the car wasn't parked in front.*

*Sometimes they put the car in the garage, sometimes they left it outside. It always changed. I judged by the time of day.*

*So you went to see them.*

*Yes, I rang the doorbell. It was the boy who answered.*

*He let you in, told you that his parents weren't back yet, and suggested you wait for them. Is that right?*

*Yes, that's right. He was sitting at the table in the living room. He was having a snack.*

*Good, go on.*

*I stayed standing in the hallway.*

*Why didn't you go into the living room? You knew the house well.*

*I don't know. . . . I didn't feel welcome anymore with all the money issues between us.*

*What happened next?*

*The oldest one called down from the second floor to ask her brother who it was. "It's the neighbor," he said. "He wants to talk to Mom and Dad." She went, "Again! I'm gonna call Mom and tell her." She didn't speak to me, say hello, nothing.*

*That bothered you?*

*Well, yeah.*

*Did you know her well?*

*She used to come over to play with my daughters a lot. She would call me by my first name. The two younger ones always called me Mr. Guillot, but not the oldest. The oldest one would say Constant.*

*Go on.*

*I heard her call her mother on the phone, tell her I was there and that I was waiting for them. Her mother answered that it would be better for me to come back the next day, that there was heavy traffic on the way back, that they would definitely be late. Then they talked about dinner. Her mother asked her to take a lasagna out of the freezer and warm it up. The girl hung up and told me what her mother had told her.*

*All that from upstairs.*

*Yes, she was leaning over the railing. All I could see was her long hair dangling.*

*What happened next?*

*I told her that I'd rather wait.*

*How did she react?*

*She sighed and then she said, "Mom doesn't want you to stay."*

*"I don't care," I said.*

*She answered, "I'm gonna call Mom back." She did. She hung up. She yelled, "Mom said go ahead and wait if you want, but she won't have time to talk to you to-night!" I said that I didn't care, and I stayed in the hall-way. It was starting to get dark. From where I was, I could see the boy sitting at the living room table. The light from the lamps was dim. He was drinking through a straw, sucking on it hard, and then sometimes he would blow into the milk to make bubbles.*

*Why are you lingering over those details?*

*I don't know. . . .*

*Continue, Mr. Guillot.*

*The oldest one's telephone rang. It was her mother again. The girl answered with yes or no. And then I heard her say, "No, that man's still here." Right after, before hanging up, she said, "I love you, too, Mom."*

*What were you thinking at that moment?*

*She said "that man." That's . . . that's hard to hear, you know. . . . I thought to myself that they didn't respect me, that they were surely used to talking about me like that.*

*That's what you were thinking?*

*Yes. . . . I was standing in a corner of the hallway, like I'd come begging, when I'd actually come to get back the money they stole from me! I crossed my hands behind my back and I stared at my feet in the dark. That's when a huge wave of fatigue hit me.*

*How so?*

*I felt as though all my energy was draining away. Like I was being crushed.*

*Like you were tired of everything?*

*Yes, that's it, and disgusted, too.*

*With what?*

*With myself.*

*And after?*

*The oldest one's phone rang again. She picked up. Her mother. I heard her say that she had finished her homework, that her brother was having his snack in the living room, and that her sister was playing quietly in her room. There was silence—she was listening to her mother on the phone. Then she said, "No, he's still here, Mom, but we didn't let him in. He's waiting by the door." She hung up, then she yelled, still from upstairs, "Mom and Dad will be here in twenty minutes!" And that's when something happened that kind of . . . let's say, it made me lose it.*

*What happened? Try to be specific, please, it's important.*

*I'll try. . . . She put her phone in the back pocket of her jeans. Then she gathered her hair behind her neck with one hand calmly, like this. She glared at me, then she stretched out her lower jaw as far as she could. All the muscles in her face were tensed. It looked like she was going to go for my throat and bite me.*

*She was provoking you. . . .*

*That's not how I took it.*

*How did you take it?*

*It was like she wanted to show me who was boss, put me in my place.*

*A twelve-year-old child?*

*Twelve is old enough to understand those things.*

*Go on.*

*In that moment, I thought to myself that I didn't*

*impress anyone, not even a twelve-year-old girl. I was nothing to them. They were for sure going to send me home, and I would never see my money again. I'd lost from the start.*

*Did that anger you?*

*I felt hatred, overwhelming hatred, rising and rising. I couldn't control it anymore. I closed my eyes and . . .*

*And . . . ?*

*And then the idea to do it popped into my head. I thought to myself that twenty minutes was more than enough for what I had to do.*

*Do what, Mr. Guillot? Be specific, please, even though I understand exactly what you meant.*

*Kill. I had to do it, it was the only solution.*

*The only solution to what?*

*I don't know, the solution to the whole mess. I wanted it to be over.*

*You weren't able to calm yourself down?*

*It was too late. It was like every part of me was leaking out.*

*Earlier, you said that you hadn't slept in three days. Do you think that could have played a role in your loss of control?*

*Maybe, yes. I was exhausted. All I could think about was the money that had been stolen from me.*

*Why the children?*

*If I killed them, it would kill their parents.*

*Your paternal instinct didn't reason with you?*

*I couldn't think, much less reason.*

*You wanted revenge.*

*I wanted to hurt them.*

*Because of eight thousand euros?*

*They weren't taking me seriously. They were humiliating me.*

*And that didn't seem absurd to you? Excessive?*

*I was in a rage.*

*A rage?*

*Yes.*

*What does that mean to you, Mr. Guillot, "a rage"?*

*You stop thinking, you're choking, you need air.*

*You wanted to get justice for yourself?*

*Maybe.*

*At that moment, you weren't planning on killing the parents?*

*No, only the children.*

*Go on, please.*

*Without thinking I went into the living room. The*

*kid looked at me, surprised but not scared. I took the bat from where it was next to the fireplace.*

*You went there directly?*

*Yes, I know the house by heart. He always puts his bat in that same spot.*

*You mean to say Mr. Langlois?*

*Yes.*

*And then?*

*I picked up the bat and held it like this, with both hands. I went closer to the boy and I hit him hard at the back of the neck.*

*Did he see you grab the bat?*

*Yes, but then he looked back into his bowl. He was playing with his straw, blowing bubbles with it. He wasn't worried at all.*

*What did you feel after you killed him?*

*Nothing.*

*Nothing?*

*In the moment, nothing. It was like I was a spectator.*

*Watching yourself?*

*Yes, exactly.*

*Did you realize he was dead immediately?*

*Yes.*

*How?*

*I recognized death, is all.*

*You'd already seen someone dead?*

*That was the first time.*

*Then how could you be so sure?*

*Instinct. I just knew.*

*Do you think, Mr. Guillot, that the instinct that allowed you to recognize death was the same one that drove you to kill?*

*I don't understand the question.*

*When people talk about instinct, it's generally in reference to animals.*

*I'm less than an animal. An animal never kills unnecessarily.*

*That's not what I said, Mr. Guillot. Did you feel unburdened somehow, when you acted? Disembodied?*

*Disembodied?*

*Yes, an out-of-body experience, if you prefer.*

*I dunno.*

*Did you feel powerful?*

*A little . . .*

*Like God?*

*I dunno, I'm not religious.*

*You could finally act on what had happened?*

*Yes.*

*Did killing the members of the Langlois family bring you a feeling of justice?*

*In the moment, a little, I think.*

*And after?*

*It's torture.*

*Meaning?*

*They're always with me. The children especially. I see them at night, covered in blood, in their clothes. During the day, I hear them breathing.*

*That must be terrifying.*

*I'm in hell.*

*Do you regret your actions?*

*I lost control. . . . I lost my mind. I . . .*

*Mr. Guillot, I asked you a question: Do you regret your actions?*

*It seems obvious, doesn't it?*

*Perhaps not to everyone.*

A silence descended upon the courtroom. You opened your mouth to answer the judge's question, but your body slipped to the side, your eyes rolled backward, and you fell abruptly to the foot of your chair. A heavy thud. You had lost consciousness.

When the trial resumed, you explained how you had

killed the two other children, then the parents. Your lawyers looked tense. The account of the parents' murder inevitably supported the premeditation argument.

At the end, the prosecutor said, *If I heard what Mr. Guillot said correctly, before he passed out, he killed five members of the same family because of a twelve-year-old girl who didn't deign to say hello to him and who, he believes, almost bit him! At least that's how he interpreted it. A killing spree triggered by nothing more than a child making a face! Mr. Guillot therefore murdered because of an error in judgment. A misunderstanding. Mr. Guillot spilled blood because of a mirage.*

A few people in the room laughed. The prosecutor went on to underline your immaturity, your intolerance for frustration, and your unhealthy inability to put things into perspective. You just blinked. You stared at your hands on your knees, like you were talking to them. You were no longer listening. I think that, like me, you were thinking about that word: *mirage*.

hen the holidays approached, Bakary invited us to celebrate what he called Friend Christmas—a family tradition established by his parents that he had maintained, year after year. A few days before they went to visit Sylvia's family for Christmas Eve, Bakary would invite over their closest friends. Everyone brought one or more small gifts (though never anything expensive) that they placed beneath the Christmas tree, and Bakary would hand them out randomly after dinner. More than anything else, it was a celebration of friendship, a chance to gather once a year and enjoy one another's company— the holiday without all its commercial trappings.

But that year Bakary had put off getting in touch

with his friends. The move that had occupied his time and thoughts had also disrupted his routines and shifted his priorities. When he finally made up his mind to call them, it was too late. No one was available. Aware that distance doesn't facilitate spontaneous initiatives, Bakary resigned himself to them not coming. Everyone, without exception, had promised to come the following Christmas.

Bakary then decided to gather his *new friends* for a meal. There was no denying we were his second choice, so when he invited us, I almost declined. But the fact that he was so eager to be nice to us made me change my mind. He was as enthusiastic about the upcoming celebration as if we had been longtime friends. He also invited Lucie and Simon, whose kindness and spontaneous wedding invitation he hadn't forgotten. Plus François, who he had gotten to know at the Tennessee, where he would grab coffee every morning before starting the workday.

The party was set for Saturday, December 19. Bakary asked us to dress up—that was part of the tradition, too, and to be completely honest, we weren't too excited about it. We gave in, anyway. You put on the only suit you owned, and I the only evening attire in my closet: a long strappy dress. Our two daughters wanted to wear makeup. I said yes to glittery eye shadow, no to lipstick.

When the door to the chalet opened that night, the delicious smell of braised meat, rosemary, melted chocolate, and orange peels immediately whetted our appetites. The warmth inside contrasted so dramatically with the winter cold that the mere act of switching from one to the other felt like crossing the border into a foreign country.

Bakary and Sylvia welcomed us together. He was wearing a royal-blue suit that accentuated his physique perfectly. The jacket clung tightly to his shoulders, giving him an electrifying overall appearance of strength and good health. Sylvia had on a pure silk dress with a small slit on the side that revealed part of her legs. On her right ankle, a chain with thin links dangled to her white foot. Her feet were bare, which surprised me. Undoubtedly sensing that I was taken aback, she told me with a mischievous smile, *I never wear shoes when I'm at home. I hope it doesn't bother anyone.*

I assured her, blushing a little, that it wasn't a big deal. Their two little girls were wearing turquoise dresses, simultaneously elegant and simple, and silvery ballet flats. The boy had on a white short-sleeved dress shirt and blue khakis.

We were the first to arrive. The living room was bathed in a gentle, pleasant light. Music was coming from somewhere. In one corner, a meticulously decorated tree blinked and projected flashes of light onto the ceiling and the white walls. There were lots of small, prettily wrapped presents around the base of the tree, and we added our own to the pile. A fire was burning in the fireplace. It smelled of dry wood and pine resin.

Bakary and Sylvia's children led our daughters upstairs, and we didn't see them again until the very end of the night. Sylvia had taken up cold dishes, drinks, and sweets to them.

*Two birds, one stone*, she said to us. *The children can enjoy the evening how they want, and we won't be constantly bothered.*

Unlike Sylvia, I didn't see any drawback to being *bothered* by my children. I actually kind of liked sensing them hovering nearby, like puppies clamoring to suckle. The incessant demands that children so often inundate us with, and the annoyance those demands generally provoke, add something chaotic and joyful—inseparable, in my mind, from the very definition of a party.

You settled onto the big comfortable couch. From the way you let your body sink into the soft cushions, I immediately understood that you weren't there as a guest, more like a regular. Which is exactly how Bakary treated you, asking you to come choose a bottle of wine from the cellar, to go with him to the woodshed to get a few logs, and even to change the music.

Sylvia smiled almost constantly, making endless back-and-forth trips between the kitchen and living room. I offered her my help, but she refused each time, assuring me that there wasn't much to do, which of course wasn't true. She kept an assortment of canapés and appetizers flowing to the coffee table, and every time I met her eyes, she'd wink, as if to assure me that everything was fine and I didn't need to worry about anything. Still, being forced to do nothing was hard for me to accept, especially since the amount of food left no doubt as to the time she must have already spent in the kitchen.

Simon and Lucie arrived twenty minutes after us, closely followed by François. I welcomed Simon's deep voice with a feeling of relief. I literally threw myself into his arms, to his amusement, and let out a liberating *Ah, there you are!*, which I later regretted saying in front of Sylvia as it clearly betrayed my discomfort.

In their smart clothes, Lucie, Simon, and François seemed like new people. Even I, who had balked at the idea of dressing up for a simple evening with friends, had to admit that Bakary's suggestion wasn't as ridiculous as I had thought; it actually gave us a chance to see one another differently.

Over dinner, Simon told us all kinds of hilarious stories about his neighbor, a new transplant from the city who had been growing rice in his garden for a few months.

*Just think about it, this guy was an engineer at the biggest electricity company in France, and his wife was working for a PR firm. They gave up everything to become farmers! The guy dug two big ponds in his garden to grow rice. Rice! Someone wanna tell me how much he's gonna make with those damn ponds?! Once he harvests his little grains of rice, he won't even have enough to make paella! And get this, his wife is raising "free-range" rabbits. The things are as big as baby pigs! She bought them from a Polish breeder. I've never seen them that size—mutants, basically. She built movable hutches with wire-mesh bottoms so that the rabbits can eat the grass. She moves them around all day long in their hutches—only fresh grass for those lucky bastards. The wife's burly, like a Belarusian female wrestler, you know, big, big biceps. You get a smack from her and you go straight into the ICU.*

*The trouble with those Polack rabbits is that two*

*days ago they all kicked the bucket. Not a single survi-*
*vor. She found them all the other morning, lying on their*
*backs, completely blue. A hundred dead rabbits. I mean,*
*come on, can you imagine? Fucking rabbits!*

Sylvia burst out laughing, both hands over her
mouth. François, who hadn't looked up from his plate
once as he listened, silently chuckled and slowly chewed
the scallops pan-fried with foie gras that Sylvia had prepared. Lucie smiled out of politeness, keeping her head
perfectly straight, like a countess holding court or a
mother making herself listen to her child without revealing her boredom. As for Bakary, he let out a slightly
forced laugh. It was so unlike him that I wondered if
something was spoiling his good mood—was he in
pain?—forcing him to put on a happy front so that nothing would show. I also noticed that he was paying constant attention to Sylvia, lightly brushing his hand down
her neck or over her hair, which she had arranged over
her right shoulder and which was hanging down to the
tip of her breast. She seemed to be ignoring her husband,
as if his caresses were a mere effect of the wind.

After dinner, Bakary, whose good mood seemed to
have been restored, suggested we have coffee in the living room.

Simon sprawled on the couch, dramatically patting

his stomach: *Rub-a-dub-dub, thanks for the grub, Mrs. Langlois!*

We all echoed the sentiment. Sylvia was inarguably a pro in the kitchen.

Lucie snorted. *Why are you calling her "Mrs. Langlois"?*

Simon pinched the tip of Lucie's nose between his fingers and pulling it from one side to the other told her, *C'mon, my pretty little love muffin—it's a joke!*

Bakary added some wood to the fireplace, then, turning toward his wife, invited her to dance. She followed him without a word.

She appeared tiny in his arms. He squeezed her against him, enveloping her so that she disappeared completely. All we could see were her bare feet. They danced with erotic insolence, paying us no mind at all. Because the orientation of the couch allowed no other viewpoint, we found ourselves forced to watch something we would have preferred not to. We were trapped. Simon attempted a joke, but we were done laughing.

Yet even as we found ourselves sinking into a bottomless pit of awkwardness, you stared at them with a stony, somewhat terrifying neutrality, without ever looking away. Did they fascinate you? Unsettle you? I couldn't figure out what the sight of their two interlaced bodies

was stirring up inside of you. Their increasingly sugges-
tive swaying finally made us all look away. You were
the only one who didn't. It was as though you were chal-
lenging them, standing your ground, alternating between
desire and aversion, marvel and consternation. We could
hear the children running up and down the hallway upstairs, and that tangible reminder that they were there,
existing somewhere outside of us, made me feel like I was
in exile.

Finally the music stopped, forcing the couple to
separate. Sylvia ran her hands through her hair, now a
little undone, and Bakary, as if pulled from a long slumber, gave an endless sigh that seemed to express all the
annoyance he felt at having to release his wife.

All of a sudden, he clapped loudly and suggested
we open the gifts. The relief was universal. Bakary put
the music back on and Sylvia sat cross-legged near the tree,
revealing a little more of her thighs. I caught François peek-
ing, timidly lingering on her white skin. I looked away.

Sylvia randomly assigned the gifts, and Bakary handed
them out. There was an assortment of trinkets: scented
candles, scented pens, bath pearls, key rings, soap, shaving cream, a bottle opener, toothpicks, sparkly lip gloss,
novelty beer coasters, a lavender sachet, Irish beer, and so
on. François ended up with the sparkly lip gloss and me

the shaving cream. We all refused to exchange our gifts. François said we had to give fate a chance, and that if he got the lip gloss, it was because there was someone to offer it to. I added that I, not immune from a surge of hair growth, would carefully hold on to my shaving cream. That made François laugh, chasing away the sad shadows brought on by the reference to his loneliness. François had lost his wife six years earlier to leukemia. The time it had taken for him to recover from that terrible experience hadn't diminished his thirst for life or our shared hope of seeing him remarry one day.

The music stopped again, but we didn't notice. The fire was crackling; we stared at it, mesmerized. The wind caught in the doorsills was whistling.

A discussion about our respective careers began. I hadn't held a job since my children had been born, but for some time—no doubt because my daughters had reached reasonable ages, three and six—I'd surprised myself with a renewed desire to work, though in a completely different field from the one I'd been trained for. After spending a few months in the maternity ward, I had realized that childcare didn't interest me as much as I had hoped. Once again, as with nursing school, I'd grown bored. It was a fairly low-paying job, and one that took up a lot of time. Sometimes, I also think that a career I had chosen because I loved children lost its appeal once I became a mother myself.

Sylvia mentioned how hard it was for her to balance her career and her family life. She couldn't manage, she told us.

*Actually, speaking of, if anyone knows someone willing to help me around the house, I'm all ears.*

*You're looking for someone to clean?* asked Lucie.

*Yes,* answered Bakary. *The house is big, and we can't find the time to take care of it.*

Sylvia furrowed her brows and mockingly said, *What do you mean "we"?*

Bakary burst out laughing and admitted, a little abashed, to not carrying all his weight when it came to housework.

Lucie said that Simon helped her a lot, and that in fact he was an excellent *househusband.* Simon winked at her and, planting a big kiss on her round cheek, said, as if he was talking to a baby being tucked in: *You truly are my little love muffin.*

I don't know how the idea came to me or why it came to me. It came to me is all. I said, without even thinking, *I'm interested.*

You were sitting next to me, our knees and thighs touching. Bakary looked at me like he was waiting to see what would happen next. He remained silent, gave an inquisitive smile, then looked at his wife, who herself didn't know exactly what was going on. Finally he said, *You?*

I said, *Yes, me, I'm interested.*

In that second, I felt you stiffen. You said nothing, you didn't move, but your tense muscles on the verge of snapping seemed to say everything that refused to come out of your mouth. I repeated, *Yes, I'm interested.*

Bakary smiled even wider and, turning his head toward you, not noticing the extreme tension in your body, said, *Why not?*

*True*, added Sylvia, without giving you time to respond. *It has its advantages. You live across from us. We know you. We trust you completely. Actually, it would be perfect!*

Simon listened, seeming uncomfortable. Lucie and François didn't say anything.

*It would let me work without the constraints of a full-time job*, I explained, *and give me some autonomy.*

Bakary and Sylvia said that it was a great idea and that they didn't know why they hadn't thought of it earlier. On the spot, we picked a time to discuss the administrative formalities, then we drank to our health and to the *wonderful idea*!

You were riled up the whole night. In the days that

followed, you reproached me repeatedly for not talking to you about it beforehand, for acting like you didn't exist, and for betraying you.

*You could have looked for a job somewhere else*, you kept saying, sweeping your hand across your forehead as if you were checking for a fever. *Why their house? Cleaning lady for the neighbors! Why their house?*

You seemed to have forgotten that it had been getting harder to make ends meet at the end of the month for some time, that you complained about it constantly, and that there was an urgent need for me to do something. Plus, I didn't see anything degrading about cleaning houses, which you conceded.

*But* (you repeated over and over) *not for the neighbors, not the neighbors!*

For one week afterward you only talked to me in grunts, and when you finally starting using words again, it was to attack Bakary and rail about how insulting his idea was. You seemed to have forgotten that it was me who had suggested it first. Not him.

After a brief discussion with Sylvia, we agreed that I would come to their house three times a week. Bakary suggested drawing up a formal job offer from their company, which meant that they'd be getting me for free. Officially, I was cleaning their offices.

Sylvia had said that three hours per visit would largely suffice. I don't know if that decision was based on personal experience or a rough estimate, but the fact remained that no matter how hard I tried, I couldn't get the whole chalet done in three hours. I always finished dead tired and didn't even have enough time to clean every room. In reality, I needed closer to five hours.

I decided to talk to Sylvia about it. Not surprisingly,

she was against it at first. Increasing my paycheck, she said, would go over their projected budget. I argued that as things stood, I'd end up giving up the job. She finally agreed to extend my work hours, vaguely annoyed by what she perceived as my bad grace.

Three nights a week I'd return home exhausted with the strange and unpleasant sensation of feeling cramped in my own house, as though spending five hours in an enormous, fancy chalet had suddenly revealed to me the extent of my mediocrity. After work, I still had dinner to prepare and the girls to take care of. At their age, they were always as full of energy as when they had just woken up. My days felt never-ending.

I made sure that when you walked in, I didn't look as tired as I was; I was afraid it would set you off. But at night I fell asleep as soon as my head hit the pillow, and it was plenty clear from your sour face the next morning that you weren't fooled.

You had distanced yourself from Bakary, routinely refusing his invitations to come over on Sundays. Seeing how disappointed he'd be, you would claim that you had to prepare for an important match, which, based on the way you'd always operated (you never prepared for anything), was fairly suspicious. And yet Bakary didn't take offense. Although he could be pretty astute in any number of situations, there was something in his personality that made it hard for him to recognize conflict, or at least single out its cause, which left him as naive and vulnerable as a child. So he waited, confident and unfazed. He continued to invite you over every weekend, and it never occurred to him that the reason you weren't accepting concerned him directly.

But Sylvia wasn't fooled. One morning, she met me in the doorway and before even saying hello asked whether you were okay. Veiling my discomfort, I replied that yes, you were fine. To cut the interrogation short, I claimed that you had lots of work, that it was always the same this time of year, and that soon everything would get back to normal. She smiled, not really believing me. Moving aside to let me enter the house, she looked me up and down with no attempt to hide her deep puzzlement.

As she closed the front door, she offered me coffee before I got started. In the kitchen, she set two mugs on the table, sat down, and then, before I could even take off my coat, told me that she had forgotten the sugar. Quite naturally, I headed toward the cupboard, grabbed the sugar bowl, and placed it on the table. Sylvia didn't thank me. Her silence implied that there was no need to say anything whatsoever. I worked for her, and the clock had started. With that, she placed our relationship in a new category. Simply noticing this disconcerted me so much that I remained standing up next to the table, which didn't appear to bother Sylvia. She listed the different tasks that I was to carry out but made no mention of what had been bugging her when I arrived, meaning the friction between you and Bakary; she seemed to have forgotten about it.

In February, over the winter break, Sylvia and Bakary hosted a group of friends they hadn't seen since they'd moved. The mood in the chalet was festive and I quickly found myself overloaded with work. Cleaning a house full of people was quite the feat, especially since they were constantly underfoot. They didn't get up at the same time but occupied different rooms in turns, forcing me to wait for each one to empty before I could clean it.

A horde of hyperactive children, whom none of the adults were inclined to lecture, came and went starting first thing in the morning, not caring whether the floor was dry or wet, or even noticing my presence. A massive droopy-faced dog was constantly sprawled on the couch. It growled every time I wanted to move it, shedding and contaminating the room with a smell of wet dog that didn't seem to gross out anyone but me.

At the end of the visit, before everyone headed home, Sylvia decided to organize a party. She asked if I would help her in the kitchen and with serving. I happily agreed to the first task, but I didn't want to serve people. "Serving" went beyond my duties; I hadn't been hired for that. Seeing my mood suddenly darken, she apologized immediately, and we didn't discuss it again.

I spent the day of the party at her side and left in the evening, after helping her set the table and before the rest of the guests. Sylvia waved goodbye, smiling less than usual, and wished me a good night.

On my way home, I ran into Simon and Lucie. We kissed hello, then, with a simple head motion toward the Langlois house, Simon asked me what time I was planning to come back. I looked at him, not understanding what he meant. Then Lucie said, *You're invited to the Langloises' tonight, right?*

Before I could answer, I saw in Simon's eyes that he had understood that we weren't. His facial expression went from enthusiastic to dismayed and then, in his desperation not to react, comical. Lucie nervously touched her hair and looked at Simon in a silent plea for help. I stammered out a few words, claiming a visit to my parents, and rushed inside our house quickly, leaving them both a little lost, torn between wanting to be with the Langloises and to stay away in solidarity with us. Through the sheer curtains of our kitchen window, I saw them hurry into the chalet like the devil was at their heels.

Later, I thought back to Sylvia's proposition. Had she considered for a single second the humiliating situation I would have found myself in had I accepted it? Serving my own friends? Did she have any idea of how that would have felt? I chose not to dwell on it, telling myself she'd spoken without thinking. I chased the incident from my mind, and my confusion dissipated just as quickly, like I'd pulled out a long splinter stuck beneath my fingernail.

You were oblivious. At least that's what I hoped. I hadn't mentioned the incident, and, knowing you, you would have told me if you'd heard about it from someone else.

In the days that followed, you didn't seem any more perturbed than usual. I concluded, relieved, that nothing had reached your ears.

But then, one night as you walked in, you said to me, *Big has a new pet!*

Not understanding what you meant, I asked you to explain.

You told me you had spotted Simon and Bakary walking side by side, that it wasn't the first time, and that it had looked as if they were really close.

You laughed and pretended not to care, but your constant pacing betrayed your nerves. I pointed out that you only had yourself to blame, that if you hadn't held a grudge against Bakary, he most likely wouldn't have moved on.

You immediately objected that you didn't *give a damn about Bakary* and that everyone was free to do what they wanted. I didn't believe a word you said, and with a provocative smile, I called you a liar. You erupted in anger.

*I don't give a damn about Bakary! How many times do I have to say it? Fuck Bakary, do you get that? Fuck him!*

Your show of anger convinced me that I was right in thinking you missed Bakary and that nothing you were claiming was true. You shut yourself in the bedroom and I thought I heard you bark, *Fucking ape.*

That should have shocked me. But I didn't react. It's out of anger, I told myself. Anger. Or else, which was more likely, I had heard wrong.

One March morning, I entered the Langlois home. Normally, there'd be no one there or else, less often, Sylvia would be waiting for me before she left.

That day, I was surprised to find Bakary and Simon chatting at the kitchen table. They got up as soon as they saw me. I went over to Simon to kiss him hello. He acted embarrassed, like I'd caught him going through a dead man's pockets. Then I went upstairs to clean the bedrooms. I heard them talking but couldn't make out anything distinct.

When I came back down half an hour later, they were standing, about to part ways. Bakary, in the doorway, held out his hand to Simon, who smiled, in satisfaction it seemed. Simon said that he would think about it, and Bakary nodded. Both men set off to their respective place of work.

The following Thursday, it was Sylvia who greeted me. She was sitting at the dining room table looking through documents and transcribing sections onto her computer.

She seemed upset, blinking nervously. She didn't see me right away. But as soon as she looked up, she smiled and greeted me warmly. The worried look in her eyes had set her black pupils dancing. That vulnerability, or turmoil really, which I had never seen in her before, moved me. Instead of working against her, her distress gave her depth.

In a soft, barely audible voice, she told me that she had a little work to finish at the house and that she would head to the office later that morning. I offered to make her coffee. *Okay*, she said, *but only if you have some with me.* I brought over two mugs. She thanked me with a slight nod and offered me a seat. I asked her if everything was okay. She answered yes. *Yes, yes, yes.* After that, not another word. She stirred her coffee, lifting her head occasionally, like someone behind me was calling her. Finally, she sighed weakly and whispered into the silence, *What a nightmare . . .*

I didn't say anything. I didn't know if I was meant

to notice or do the opposite—ignore her. Was she aware that I had heard her or was she so deeply lost in thought that she hadn't even realized what she said? Either way she abruptly sat up straight and, slamming one hand on the table, said, *C'mon!* I quickly understood she was talking as much to me as to herself, which is why I stood right away.

In a more assured tone Sylvia told me it would be good to clean the windows that day, that they needed it. I said okay and headed to the kitchen. Sylvia called me back and, holding out the two empty mugs, asked me to put them in the dishwasher and start a cycle.

Later that morning, after she threw on her coat and before she could open the door, her telephone rang. It was Bakary. After only a few seconds, her voice brightened. *That's amazing. That's so amazing. Well done, my love, bravo.* She yelled out, *Bye, Anna, I'm off!* I was in the second-floor bathroom. *Bye, Sylvia!* That same night, as I was closing the shutters in our kitchen, I saw Simon and Lucie go into the Langloises' house.

The next evening, you called to tell me you were going to grab a drink at the Tennessee, with Simon.

You came home a little after nine and announced that Simon had placed thirty thousand euros in a Swiss account.

*One of Bakary's clients works in finance. He's offering really advantageous investments at low rates. All you have to do is place your money and let it work on its own. Simon is happy. He's sure that he's gonna make a killing!*

I was surprised by the amount that Simon had decided to invest.

*An inheritance*, you told me. *His grandmother left him a good chunk of change.*

Since I still didn't understand why he had invested so much money, you explained that the more he put in, the more he would make.

*Bakary made him guarantees?* I asked.

You reassured me on that point, claiming that he had Simon sign official documents and that everything was in order. You added that François was considering investing money, too.

Then I was surprised to notice that you seemed a lot less angry with Bakary. It was as though this business with financial investments had erased your bitterness toward him just like that.

When our conversation ended, leaving each of us to our own silent thoughts, I detected a faint look of distress in your eyes. You were pensive the whole night. We were sitting on the couch, in front of the television, when

I realized that your eyes weren't focused on anything. You were there without being there, mulling something over. I knew you well enough that I could guess what was weighing on your mind and follow, all too closely, your train of thought.

It was noon on a Sunday, after a visit to your parents. You sat down at the table looking like a man up to no good and said, *I'm gonna invest some cash, too!*

Our bank account was bone-dry and I didn't see by what miracle you would go about getting the money. I looked away and acted like I hadn't heard anything. I didn't want to talk about that money business in front of our children.

There was a whiff of mutiny in the air. Our daughters were refusing to eat their Brussels sprouts. *They smell like butts*, protested one, while the other plugged her nose.

I snapped, *If you don't finish your meal, there'll be no dessert and no treats!*

The girls looked at each other and, without a word, resigned themselves to their fate. I had hit where it hurt. They shoved down the vegetables without chewing, accompanying every swallow with a face of disgust and an *eww* intended to illustrate their sacrifice.

Exasperated by their little game, I begged you to make them stop. You did nothing. In fact, the joking seemed to amuse you. *It's no big deal, honey bunny. We're allowed to have fun every once in a while.*

Honey bunny. That's what you called me. Honey bunny. I was so surprised that I stopped eating mid-bite.

*Well, what? Did I say something wrong?* you asked me. The girls snickered. And you went and made bunny ears over your head.

For a brief moment, I had the unpleasant sensation that everything was slipping away from me, that I was completely out of sync. Like my life was falling apart and I couldn't salvage any of it. But I composed myself immediately and, glaring at you, asked what you were playing at. You couldn't find anything to say but *Bunnies are cute, honey bunny.* Of course, the girls burst out laughing.

Sensing I was about to explode, you gave them a stern look and demanded silence with one finger over your mouth. They stared at you to figure out if your anger was real or made-up. They let a few giggles slip, torn between suspicion and excitement, then, quickly understanding that you weren't serious and that you weren't upset with them, they agreed to calm down so as not to rile me up again. After dessert, to my relief, they left the table.

As soon as we were alone, I pressed you to tell me about the money we didn't have but that you said you wanted to invest.

*I have money,* you told me, *my parents agreed to lend me some.*

*How much?* I asked.

*Eight thousand euros.*

*Eight thousand euros? That's a lot.*

*Yeah, I know, but the more you invest, the more profit you make.*

*Okay . . . but why are you doing this?* I didn't understand.

*I already told you, I'm investing!*

*But what for?* I asked calmly. *There's no need to. It's not even your money. . . .*

You stiffened and your eyes widened. It was like you'd just lit up a room that had been plunged in darkness. Then you said: *My parents agree. I told them about the financial investments. They think it's a good thing. With what it's gonna make us, I'll be able to pay them back, no problem, and make a profit from the interest.*

*I'm guessing that's all of their savings . . . isn't it?*

You nodded yes, as though you were afraid to hear yourself say it. I looked at you. I couldn't figure out what was motivating you. Money had never interested you, and this investment plan struck me as antithetical to the sense of integrity that had guided your life and ours. I pointed out that your parents weren't rich and that I thought it was stupid to ask them for all of their savings to invest. *What if it doesn't work?*

You assured me that Simon was very pleased with his investment; that, only two weeks after he'd placed his money in the account, Bakary had assured him that it was already paying off and he had nothing to worry about. You had run into Bakary that morning and he was expecting you that afternoon to discuss the plan. You hadn't said a word to him in weeks and there you were, not hesitating for a second to approach him about some financial investment! You were acting as if you'd forgotten everything—me getting hired by the Langloises, the humiliation you had felt, the anger that had been so hard for you to get rid of. . . . When I pointed all of that out, you dismissed it with one sweep of your hand: *You should be happy I'm not bitter!*

I was speechless. All of a sudden, my housekeeping job—which, judging from your fits of rage, had verged on being a federal case—had lost all importance to you. It was as if nothing had ever happened.

That night, after you saw Bakary, you were different. The glazed look in your eyes betrayed your anxiety. You seemed to be fighting some prolonged battle with your own thoughts. You had made a deal with Bakary, but I sensed something was dampening your enthusiasm.

You got yourself a glass of water from the faucet, which you drank to the last drop, head tilted way back. Then, slightly out of breath, you said, *He hesitated, dammit. He hesitated before he took it. . . .*

You put your glass in the sink, looked at me without blinking, and told me that Bakary had seemed disappointed with the amount you wanted to invest.

*I don't see how it's his business!* I responded, appalled. *You invest the amount you can!*

Your shock at Bakary's disdain had cast a shadow over your face. *He hesitated*, you said, over and over, *he hesitated.*

*Of course he hesitated*, I yelled. *We're far from Simon's thirty thousand euros!*

I was furious then, and today still, in light of everything that happened, Bakary's reaction leaves a bad taste in my mouth. Why did he have to turn up his nose knowing that he would, quite clearly, eventually accept the money that he urgently needed? Why the theatrics? Why choose to humiliate you when he could have easily avoided it?

Same as the night before, we spent the evening in front of the television. The volume was loud, but I could still hear the rumbling of your thoughts. You were swinging back and forth between the certainty that you'd made a good deal and the acute pain caused by Bakary's condescending attitude.

One evening, after I'd spent five hours cleaning the chalet, Sylvia told me that she couldn't guarantee my wages for the next two months. They'd had to do some renovations at their agency and the cost of that update had forced them to reduce their expenses. I was the collateral damage of their austerity plan. She nonetheless promised to hire me again after those two months and apologized for putting me in a difficult position. That's the expression she used: *a difficult position.*

Sylvia served me a strong espresso and, as sole consolation, patted me on the hand. I took the news calmly and with some relief. In reality, I couldn't stand the job anymore. It was time for me to find some real work, not that cleaning their house wasn't real, not at all; it was far more real than any other job, but I needed to find something "sustainable" and to think about what I really wanted to do with my life.

That night I told you what had happened. You had as much trouble understanding the news of my getting fired as you had when I got hired.

*Renovations? Why are they renovating? And they're letting you go for that?*

You picked up the phone to discuss it with them, but I stopped you right away. I assured you that it wasn't a big deal, that on the contrary it was a good thing and that it would allow me to find a more appealing job. *Worst-case scenario*, I said, *I won't have a hard time finding a few hours cleaning for other clients.* Finally, I asked you to stop your endless meddling in my business and told you that it was starting to seriously annoy me.

*I'm a responsible adult—not a child!*

You gave me a long stare, then, like back when you used to tell me *I love you so so much*, you took me in your arms and held me against your chest. I buried my face in your armpit and I inhaled the smell of your sweat. Deeply. It was your smell, but it was also no longer your smell. There was a whiff of something bitter, like it had soured.

*T*he carnival arrived in late August. Like every year, a large platform had been set up in the village square.

That summer, the heat was suffocating. The river had dried up, and the pine trees, burned by the sun, looked like prickly black scarecrows. It was so hot that the old men of the village slept during the day and emerged at night. As soon as the sun set, we would see them hobbling down the road. The old ladies, however, would gather at the chapel in the afternoon. *We're going to pray*, they'd say. They went in small groups, carrying handbags and smelling of eau de cologne. They would remain seated for hours on the wooden benches, gossiping quietly. Thanks to the moisture-retaining stones, the women could finally breathe; their bones would straighten out in astonishment, for a few hours. If anyone came through the large oak door, the women would freeze and stare at the figure of Christ with utter seriousness. Then they would go back to whispering beneath the cross, cheerful, liberated.

The owner of the bumper cars had arrived. He parked his trailer under the tall chestnut tree, like every year. His beautiful wife, seated on a folding chair, was examining her painted nails, spreading her fingers wide. Her dizzying cleavage created an erotic swell, prompting quivers even from the tree branches she was sitting under. She was the reason the teenagers all came.

*Check out that pair of titties.*

*They're fake.*

*No way, fuckwit.*

*Shut it.*

*Dumbfuck.*

*Shut it.*

*You've never even touched a girl.*

*Shut it, you little bitch.*

*Go get Mama 93 to suck you off.*

*Still better than getting assfucked by Abbott and Costello.*

*Dickwad . . .*

That's what we'd hear, with a few variations, whenever we walked past them. They'd set off before midnight on their noisy mopeds, promising to meet up the next day, same place, same time, not forgetting their evening farewell: *Good luck humping your dog, asshole!*

The night of the village festival, the air was warm and humid. A large tent had been erected in the common field and long tables covered with white paper were set up around it. Since that morning, the women of the village (the same ones always glued to the chapel benches) had been busy preparing a gigantic cabbage soup.

Every year, more than two hundred people would come, including those from the neighboring villages. After eating the soup, folks would hit the dance floor set up in the square. Children would go on endless bumper car races as they sucked Orangina through a straw and licked Frizzy Pazzy crystals beneath paper lanterns stretching from one tree to another.

People began arriving in the early evening. Sausages and cabbage were steaming in crusted casserole dishes, black from overuse. The aproned cooks had magenta throats and fog-coated glasses. They were stirring the soup with long steel spoons and serving it with ladles as big as a baby's head.

We had met up with Simon and Lucie, who had

wonderful news to share with us. François, however, couldn't get away from the bar. On festival nights, he would calculate his quarterly earnings.

When we arrived, Simon and Lucie were already sitting at a table. From the tender glances Simon was casting at his wife's stomach, we understood immediately. Through silent agreement, we acted as though we hadn't guessed anything. When Simon told us that Lucie was four months pregnant, and that it was a boy, we feigned surprise to such perfection that Simon, hearing our exclamations of joy, began to cry. Lucie, baffled no doubt by her husband's tears, shrugged, a little embarrassed, but moved all the same by this big, robust man turned to mush by the simple announcement of a child on the way.

When the Langloises joined us, we told them the news. Bakary hugged Simon and lifted him off the ground. Sylvia took Lucie's hand, placed it in her palm, and, smiling like a woman who knows plenty about motherhood, whispered that she was happy for her.

Then we headed to the tent where the soup was simmering. The hot air filled with the steam of boiled cabbage and fried onions. The children followed, cheerfully hopping behind us like cats that had been promised the head of a fresh sardine.

We got in line under the tent. The women were serv-

ing the soup in large bowls that they filled without looking, continuing their conversations all the while. Every
time the ladle hit ceramic, they would smile even wider.
It was so hot that they were gulping down water every
five minutes and fanning their faces with pieces of ripped
cardboard.

Simon asked for a double serving of sausage for
Lucie, but Lucie, rolling her eyes, said in her childlike
voice that she wouldn't let herself be bossed around.
*Come on, I'm not Moby Dick!*

Simon burst out laughing and handed her an overflowing bowl in which two enormous, glistening sausages, several chunks of pork, and spareribs as pink as
Madagascar shrimp were floating among the cabbage
leaves and whole potatoes. *Here you go, my little whale.
Starting today, no more counting calories!*

Once we were seated, Simon couldn't stop beaming.
Whenever he looked over at Lucie, his eyes shone with
held-back tears, and we could almost see his heart
thumping beneath his Hawaiian shirt. Lucie devoured
her meal before his emotional gaze and licked each of
her fingers, laughing.

The children rolled around on the lush grass. They
hadn't touched anything or at most ate a few soft bread
rolls, one-fourth of a sausage, a boiled potato.

Bakary and Sylvia were holding hands, like they were worried about being separated. But Sylvia wasn't all there. Something seemed to be preoccupying her. Her face would brighten then darken, repeatedly, with no visible external reason for her mood changes.

By then, every single one of the tables was taken. A few feet away from us, Abbott and Costello, accompanied by their wives, were all gussied up. They were wearing the same suits as in previous years. You could tell from the slightly worn fabric that they had lost their original color. Sitting close together, shoulder to shoulder, the pair roared with laughter, toasting with Suze. Abbott's wife had gone to the salon, her hair rippling beneath a layer of hairspray so thick it could have been taken for wood varnish. Costello's was wearing a mustard-yellow sateen dress and a straw hat that made her look a bit rakish.

After the meal, Simon suggested a few rounds of bumper cars to the kids. Whoops of delight echoed through the fairground. Sylvia begged the children to quiet down, but Simon, blissfully happy, told her that they were certainly allowed to shout and that nothing, on festival day, should be off-limits to them. In reality, he was talking about himself.

We headed toward the rides. The carny's wife, no-nonsense, heavy makeup, cloaked in perfume, was at the register. Around the track, boys of every age had their eyes glued to her cleavage. Her husband, making sure nothing interrupted the ballet of bumper cars, dashed around collecting tokens and bringing back vehicles left on the side of the track. He was sweating bullets because of the heat, and his arms—pushing, pulling, towing— were swollen with veins.

The children rushed at the miniature cars. They mounted in pairs and, unsurprisingly, whoever was lucky enough to grab the wheel first would refuse to let go, prompting disappointment in their passenger, who, frustrated at not being the driver, would cry, turn bright red, and scream that the next round would be their turn and their turn only! The children went on round after round, which eventually annoyed all of the adults except for Simon, who was completely amped up, encouraging the race car drivers and hopping around the track like a kid to music by Maître Gims, Céline Dion, and Drake.

When it got dark, Bakary suggested grabbing drinks from the refreshment stand and then going to dance. At first we had a hard time getting the kids off the track, but once we offered them cones of churros, they leaped out of their cars.

We watched them run on ahead. I remember worrying that we would see them disappear just as quickly. I sped up so that I wouldn't lose sight of them; there were lots of people. When I turned around to make sure the group was still following us, I caught your eye. You gave me a sad and angry look, as if you were reproaching me for something. I didn't immediately understand. Once I realized that you were walking by yourself between our paired-off friends, both couples holding hands, it was already too late to restore the balance. I continued to chase after the children, heart sinking, pace accelerating.

At the sweets stand, I had time to buy churros and drinks for all of the children. When the rest of the group finally caught up, you didn't spare me the slightest glance. Bakary gently lectured me: *Anna, you should have let me pay.*

You cut in, responding somewhat abruptly, *And why's that? We can afford to pay!* Your voice was unrecognizable. Hoarse. Almost a bark. Bakary leaned backward slightly and said that's not what he meant. His response annoyed you even more, because it implied that your feelings had been hurt.

Simon suddenly lifted his arms and said, *How about we go dance?* It wasn't a real question, more an order that didn't expect a response. Without thinking twice, we followed him to the dance floor, the children, too, swept along by music the DJ was sending into the speakers.

The DJ was a short, chubby guy, forty-five or so, with round, oily cheeks. His blue eyes, two aquamarine crystals, were spinning in every direction. And he was sliding around, too, from one turntable to another, with incredible smoothness. I wondered whether he was on roller skates. His energy was overflowing, seemingly impossible to channel. He yelled out in English, *Get down, everybody, come on, you can dance!*, bopping his head. He wasn't that young anymore and yet, on his little stage, in front of his mix table, the exact spot where the moon was shining its brightest, he was eternal.

His voice, which carried an impressive distance, attracted more and more dancers; so many that, in no time, the floor was packed. People were literally throwing themselves onto it. They began to gyrate as they set foot in a world where the body no longer obeyed anything but the urgent compulsion to move. We mirrored everyone else—we threw ourselves onto the dance floor. Our children hanging from our hips laughed from being shaken around, letting out joyful shouts. I edged closer to everyone so that I wouldn't lose you all in the crowd. The brief altercation between you and Bakary had been erased from our minds. At least that's how it seemed. Simon, who had placed himself behind Lucie, was hugging her waist. His large hands were holding her belly like he was worried it would fall off.

When the first notes of ABBA's *Dancing Queen* echoed through the square, our eyes lit up with spontaneous joy. Everyone, without exception, recognized the song immediately. An enthusiastic *ah!* rang out in unison, and our bodies straightened up in a burst of energy. There are certain songs that transport us, though we never know quite where they've taken hold. *Dancing Queen* is one of them. That was the first time that the six of us had danced together to that song, but it awakened something inside all of us as instantaneously and dramatically as a photo from our youth. The song symbolized what we had lost. That shared nostalgia reminded us that we were all navigating this world at the same time. And navigating the world at the same time isn't nothing, when you think about it. In a swell of harmony, without taking our eyes off one another, we began to dance with abandon. Each time we chanted the chorus, we were actually proclaiming our love and desperate desire for eternity. We had never been closer than in that instant, and if *Dancing Queen* could have played until the end of time and protected us from the harshness of reality, we never would have had to endure what was to come.

Sadly, songs don't last forever. When they suddenly come to an end, the cruelty of the world returns and we have to continue without the music. Now, when I think back to that moment, tears rise, and I can't help but see it as a prelude to tragedy.

Later that evening, when we were all, except for Lucie, reasonably tipsy, we—you and me—saw Bakary and Simon having a violent argument not far from the refreshment stand. Simon had grabbed Bakary by his shirt collar and yelled something that we couldn't hear because of the music. I remember giving you a questioning look. You were about to step in when Simon pushed Bakary so hard that I was afraid his head would hit the tree he was stumbling in front of.

When they rejoined us after, they acted like nothing had happened.

For the first time since I'd met him, Bakary was fighting against fear. His ordinarily direct gaze was avoiding something, and his arms, which seemed to be in his way, fell lifelessly along his sides.

Everyone in the procession of witnesses said the same thing. There had been no hints that this would happen. None. How could anyone have imagined for a single second that you were capable of such savagery?

*Normal* is the word that came up the most often during your trial. *Mr. Guillot was a normal guy.* People talked about you in the past tense, as if you no longer existed. Which was no doubt the case. Sitting in the defendant's chair, you looked dead. Pale and overcome by exhaustion.

I believe that all of us, without exception, misjudged the true nature of the man we'd known for so long. Your actions were revelatory. It's terrifying to think that I, someone who lived with you day after day, didn't see anything coming. The thing is, I never once felt afraid in your presence. Either for me or for our daughters. What happened is simply incomprehensible.

On the witness stand, Simon, Lucie, and François confirmed that you were a good and honest person. When the judge asked Simon if he still considered you a friend, he hesitated for a few seconds, then answered, with a slight tremble in his voice, that yes, you were still his friend. *Yes, of course.*

Then the judge asked him to expand on that August night that kept coming up.

*You were starting to have some doubts?*

*Yes, Your Honor.*

*The night of the village festival, is that right?*

*Yes, Your Honor.*

*You don't have to call me that every time.*

*I'm sorry.*

*Don't apologize. Go on.*

*That night, Bakary and I got into a fight. It was really tense. And yeah, we were all a little drunk, but I still felt like something was up. The next day, Constant came to find me. He wanted to know what had happened between Bakary and me. I told him that he had refused to give me back my money.*

*What were his reasons for refusing to give you back the money?*

*Bakary said that the invested money couldn't be withdrawn before six months. That that's how his client's bank worked.*

*Why did you want to get back the money that you had so recently invested?*

*Because the baby was coming. That changed everything. We wanted to fix up its room, plus everything else that comes with it—everything that a baby needs. I was crazy happy, but I needed that money.*

*Did you insist on getting it back?*

*Yes. I even threatened to sue Bakary if he didn't pay me back within the week. Bakary promised to do everything in his power.*

*What happened next?*

*Bakary gave me back half the amount and promised to give me the other half in six months. "I scrambled like mad to get this money," he told me, "out of friendship for you!" He also said that the bank was doing me a favor, that it was an exception, and that I should consider myself a favored client. He made me believe that the bank didn't want to lose me, that I was important to them.*

*What was your reaction?*

*It was always the same thing with Bakary. He would sweet-talk you. He really did seem upset. . . . I chose to trust him.*

*And you weren't suspicious? It didn't occur to you that the Swiss bank didn't exist?*

*I know it might seem weird, but in the moment I didn't think about it. And then after that he offered me a drink, he patted me on the back, we talked baseball. The problem was no longer a problem. It was always that way with Bakary. . . .*

*What did Mr. Guillot say to you when you confided in him about your dispute with Mr. Langlois?*

*He wanted to get his money back, too. I remember he said, "This whole thing feels off."*

*Did you know that he had invested eight thousand euros?*

*Yes, he had mentioned it. I knew about his investment and our friend François's.*

*Do you think that Mrs. Langlois was aware of her husband's mishandling of funds?*

*I don't know, I doubt it. Bakary always made sure not to talk about it around her.*

*But she was still aware of the problems their company was having?*

*I think so. She seemed worried a lot.*

*So Mr. Guillot told you he wanted to get his money back?*

*Yes, he was determined. He was, like me, furious.*

*At the time, did you know that Mr. Langlois's company was in dire straits?*

*He never said anything to us. He acted like everything was fine, plus he kept up the same lifestyle.*

*Did Mr. Guillot go to see Mr. Langlois?*

*That same day.*

*What happened?*

*Bakary didn't give him back his money. He actually got annoyed and told him that the amount he'd been able to get for me was an exception. I know now that after giving me back half my money, he had nothing left. He was waiting for other "clients."*

*How did Mr. Guillot react?*

*Really bad. Mr. Langlois had given me back fifteen thousand euros without too much convincing, but he refused to return the Guillot family's eight thousand euros. That made Constant crazy. Bakary told him that he would try to get him some of the money back the following month.*

*So in September.*

*That's right.*

*And then?*

*Nothing in September. Or October. Each time Ba-
kary had the same response: "The bank says no. Next
month for sure . . ." End of November and still nothing.
That's when Constant lost it.*

*Did Mr. Guillot come to you to discuss what was
going on?*

*Yes, at first. I would reassure him. I'd try to reason
with him. I even offered to lend him some cash. You'll
pay me back in six months, I told him, when you get your
money back.*

*And?*

*He never wanted to. He wanted his eight thousand
euros. It had become an obsession. He was haunted by
the whole thing. It's all he thought about, all he talked
about. He was sleeping less and less. When we'd meet for
a drink at François's, we could see that he wasn't really
there.*

*Did your friend François also try to reclaim his
money from Mr. Langlois?*

*He had accepted the bank's conditions. He told us
that Bakary had been honest with us from the start by
clearly explaining that the bank would refuse to give us
back our money before six months.*

*Had he really specified that?*

*Honestly, I don't remember.*

*Were you and your friend François worried about Mr. Guillot's behavior?*

*Let's just say that we could see the situation was becoming alarming.*

*Did you help him get some perspective?*

*We tried.*

*Didn't you have any influence on Mr. Langlois? Couldn't you have gone to see him to encourage him to return Mr. Guillot's money, like he had done for you?*

*He wouldn't have given it back. He didn't have it anymore. . . .*

*Did you imagine that your friend was capable of such an outpouring of violence?*

*No, it was impossible. Not him.*

*That's a categorical no.*

*Categorical. We were all shocked the day we found out. We spent the whole night talking about it, trying to understand.*

*Who's "we"?*

*Constant's friends.*

*How do you all explain his actions?*

*We can't. But . . . sometimes, sometimes I tell myself that maybe he'd . . . been hurt.*

*By whom? By what?*

*By life, by Mr. Langlois, something like that.*

*Is that a valid reason to kill five people?*
*No, of course not. He went too far.*
*You said it. Do you have anything to add?*
*No, nothing.*
*Thank you.*

*One year after the end of the trial*

The proprietor hands me the keys. Her hands are as small as a child's.

*Room 28. It has a tub. You'll see that I left you some bubble bath. Do you like coconut? It's coconut. But subtle coconut, right, not the sugary kind that'll make you dizzy, uh-uh, it's very light, you'll see, real delicate.*

Her bright, curious smile throws me off; I don't know if it's intended for me or if it's simply the way she always looks. Suddenly she asks, *Your husband or your son?* The question sends chills through me and I freeze, panicked. Is it written on my forehead that I've come to see a prisoner? There's no way I can maintain eye contact, and with the same confusion I've felt for months, I lower my head in a sign of submission.

*Don't be embarrassed, dear. I've been hosting inmates' wives and mothers in this hotel for twenty-two years. Some come from far away, for years now. Now don't you worry. You're at home here. I won't ask you anything else.*

Because I say nothing, she gently places her hand on mine. This maternal concern demands no effort from her. Her affection comes naturally, almost as if she's on this earth to put others back together. When I feel the warmth of her skin, I choke back a sob.

*Would you like to have dinner with us tonight?* Met with my worried silence, she says, a bit quieter, like how you'd talk to a sleepwalker standing on a window ledge, *It's on the house, of course. . . . At seven, in the kitchen. I know that everyone has to get up tomorrow. Visiting hours are very early. So seven's good, right? There'll be two other people: Jeanne, who made the trip from Corsica to see her son, and Maud, same, her son. They come here every month. That's it. I'm telling you that because it's all I know about them. I promise. We never talk about anything upsetting, only what makes us happy.*

Her offer is much more than a simple dinner invitation; it's an outstretched hand that no argument could push away. I say, *Okay, I'll eat with you.* The proprietor claps. *All right, done deal,* she says, and gives me a look of such warmth that I'm this close to curling up in her arms and never leaving them.

The room is spacious. The window looks over a square lit by two streetlamps. The amenities are basic, but I immediately feel at ease. This is the first time in a long time that I've found myself alone, without the girls. And that sudden freedom, far from making me anxious, lifts a crushing weight from my daily load. I left them with my parents for a few days. I have no more responsibilities, no more duties. I can give free rein to my emotions without having to build a protective maternal wall. I can cry if I want. I'm already shaking with tears; I make no effort to hold them back. I cry, without resisting, and the simple act of hearing my sobs reminds me how much I've suffered in silence these past months.

I set my suitcase on the bed, open it, and take out my toiletries, which I place on a small shelf in the bathroom. There's a faint smell of toothpaste and household cleaner. The bathtub is spotless, smooth to the touch. I think about tomorrow and I tell myself that it will undoubtedly be a strange day, an unusual day. I haven't seen you in a year. I haven't seen anyone for that matter. When I moved more than sixty miles away from our old house, I was choosing to turn the page on everything that still connected me to our old life. The last image I have of you is from the day of the verdict. You had your back to me, a police officer on each side. The sentence had just been announced; you were crying. Life in prison. Premeditation had been established. You were crying like a lost child. What are the tears of a man who's killed five people worth? I remember that the prosecutor had paraphrased Dostoyevsky in his closing speech: *The unjust death of an innocent child makes us doubt the existence of God.* He added, *Could it make us believe in the existence of the devil? No. On second thought, Constant Guillot isn't the devil. He's much worse. An ordinary man who became a quintuple murderer.*

Your parents, who had refused to attend the trial because of the shame and unbearable pain of seeing you in the defendant's dock, nonetheless wanted to hear the verdict. On the last day of the trial, they entered the courtroom, looking thinner. Your father was holding your mother's arm tightly, as if it was about to come off. After the sentence was read, you turned around to follow the officers escorting you. Your mother held out one hand toward you, the way you'd hand a snack to a child who's forgotten their bag before they enter the classroom. That's the last time I saw them. They never again expressed a desire to see their grandchildren, as if the mere mention of them made your absence more unbearable. Neither the pain nor the love inside them will ever fade. They'll continue to love you just as deeply as before, and that feeling will probably accompany them until death, when the time comes.

I haven't seen you since that day. I haven't felt the need until now. On multiple occasions you've asked me, by mail, to bring the girls to visit, but I never agreed. I only ever allowed the exchange of letters and drawings. You will not see them. I don't want them mixed up in this anymore. I know that, deep down, you think the same thing. After your many requests, all left unanswered, I responded yes to your last one. I don't know what I expect from our meeting or why I'm taking a step in your direction. I haven't been sure of anything in a very long time.

At seven o'clock sharp, I go down to dinner. As soon as I arrive at the front desk, the proprietor leads me to the kitchen, holding my arm like I have something illegal to sell her and discretion is required.

*The girls* (she means Jeanne and Maud) *are coming. They'll be here in five minutes or so. Have a seat. I'll be right back!*

Then she walks out, leaving me alone in this kitchen that smells of rosemary and roasted meat. The table is set for five. In the center, a pitcher of cold water and a bottle of red wine. In a wicker basket, walnut bread, cut into thick slices.

The proprietor returns, followed by a young girl who must be, at most, seventeen.

*This is my daughter, Marguerite. She's just finished her homework. She's drowning in term papers this semester. Normal, right? It's her senior year!*

Visibly exhausted by her heavy workload, Marguerite greets me with a gloomy smile—or maybe it's resigned, I couldn't say—and sits at the other end of the table with a sigh, like her life is just one long string of hardships. Her blonde hair, pulled back in a ponytail, is iron straight. She's tall with legs that go on forever. Stretching one arm toward the basket, she grabs a slice of bread, then bites into it as ravenously as if she hasn't eaten in two days. Her mother, stirring vegetables and chunks of lamb in a cast-iron pot, gently chastises her without even turning around. *No, no bread, sweetheart, it'll ruin your appe-tite.* Marguerite devours the piece in a few bites, impervious to any commentary, then goes for another.

Maud and Jeanne make their entrance. The first woman looks to be about fifty, the second, a good twenty years older.

*Ah, the girls!* exclaims the proprietor, making a rapid about-turn. *Sit, sit!*

The proprietor introduces everyone by pointing at us with her spatula: *Maud, Jeanne, and . . . Mrs. Guillot, I don't know your first name. . . .*

*Anna,* I say. *My name is Anna.*

*Lovely,* she responds, turning back to her lamb stew. *Anna, she goes by Anna. We should be on a first-name basis, don't you think, my dear? Much nicer, isn't it?*

I say, *Yes, of course, much nicer.* She clearly hasn't noticed that at no point has she told me her name.

The two women take their places side by side, shoulder to shoulder, like they're worried they'll lose sight of each other. They remind me of Abbott and Costello. The thought of those two partners in crime, a memory so closely tied to a happy though now distant period in my life, breaks my heart.

Our eyes meet and though the exchange lasts barely a second, I can tell from the animalistic way we're sniffing around one another that everyone's trying to look straight into the other's soul, to divine her secrets. Jeanne, the older of the two, matches exactly the image I've always had of a Corsican woman: petite, steely-eyed, in black from head to toe. Maud is the opposite, a cheerful giantess with dyed red hair and too much makeup. When she laughs, her mouth opens wide and one shining steel tooth, an upper canine, immediately draws the gaze.

Jeanne asks Marguerite about school. The young woman answers with a yes or a no, chomping on her bread and giving a weak smile. Without even turning around (almost like she has eyes in the back of her head), the proprietor tosses out, over the steaming stew, *Come on, Marguerite, a little effort. Tell Jeanne what you did this week.*

Marguerite rolls her eyes and with as much enthusiasm as a corpse responds, *What do you want me to say?* Her ponytail whips the air with the slightest movement of her head.

Jeanne laughs. *Never mind, let her be. The youngsters don't like to talk.*

*Now that is true,* exclaims Maud. *At home, mine won't say a single word when he gets back from school.*

*You can try all you want, nothing ever comes out of that mouth. . . .*

*It's ready*, the proprietor announces suddenly. Holding the pot with both hands, she does a half-turn around herself. *Marguerite, sweetheart, quick—the trivet!*

*And voilà*, she says as she sets down the dish with as much pride as if she was tossing a stag killed during a hunt onto the center of the table. *Tonight it's stew with lamb and assorted vegetables.*

The women congratulate the chef. Maud thanks her by placing one hand over her heart and Jeanne says in appreciation, *My word, it smells so good!*

*Newbie first*, says the proprietor, looking at me. I hold out my bowl and she gives me a generous serving. Marguerite seems a little irritated at not being served first. Her ponytail whips the air again, then stops. Someone asks me where I'm from and how many hours my train ride lasted. Jeanne tells us that the trip from Corsica is long and exhausting but that she wouldn't miss her monthly visit for anything in the world.

*I'm allowed three slots of three hours, three days in a row. They change the hours if you come from far away. I brought cured sausage and capocollo, as usual!*

*I thought outside items were forbidden*, I say timidly.

*As if!*

The women tell me how to bring in goods without being bothered by the prison officials. Maud explains how at each visit, she goes in with cigarettes for her son. *You roll your cigarettes in plastic wrap, and you hide them under your armpits, using scotch tape, or around your waist, or I'm guessing you know where, don't you?!* Then she laughs, revealing her sparkling canine.

The proprietor, almost choking from laughter, coughs into her hands, hiding her mouth. Her small eyes, wet with tears, laugh on their own.

*Nobody sees anything, you know*, adds Maud, *since nobody frisks those parts of the body. They just ask you to remove everything metal: belt, jewelry, cellphone, etc. And then, well, as long as you're not bringing in drugs or a weapon, right, they basically look the other way. Cigarettes and sausages are just to make 'em feel better. They don't hurt anybody. I know my boy needs smokes, so, well, I spoil him a little. Someone has to.*

I'm worried about Marguerite's presence. It's not a conversation for a girl her age. But she doesn't seem any more perturbed than if we'd been discussing the weather. For that matter, her gaze is as bright as ever, unclouded by any visible signs of irritation. This is her world, her every day—she seems to have gotten used to it.

I'm surprised to find I have a good appetite. The proprietor gives me another serving, smiling, encouraging me to enjoy the evening with a wink. We drink wine; Maud prefers beer. *Vino gives me a headache, makes me feel like my brain's on fire.*

*Long as it's not your culo*, hoots Jeanne out of one side of her mouth.

The proprietor, who snorts at the word *culo*, almost chokes again, this time on her stew. Seized by uncontrollable giggles, Maud leans against Jeanne, who cackles just like a hyena without moving a single muscle in her face. Marguerite, with her ever flawless way of beating the air with her ponytail, sighs and, making a pained face, bends over the screen of the cellphone she grabs from her jeans pocket in one rapid movement. I laugh, too, and suddenly it becomes clear to me that everything happening tonight at this table in a kitchen that smells of rosemary was orchestrated with the sole goal of making my night a pleasant one, and to lighten the ordeal that awaits me in a few hours. Their kindness is an instinctual reaction, no doubt, triggered by still vivid memories of their first visit; that or perhaps they regret not having been on the receiving end of the same warmth and generosity they're now showing me.

I feel good. Serenity floods over me; I know it will

be short-lived, so I enjoy it as best I can. For the first time in a long time, I'm being treated like an equal. It feels like everything that was tainted by tragedy is invisible to them.

After the meal, the proprietor offers us herbal tea. *And how about we put on some music?*

*Oh, no, Mom, you're going to play us your cheesy pop again!*

Her mother gently chastises her. *Hey, missy, do I say anything to you when you play your weird music?*

Marguerite shrugs. *Electro, Mom, I already told you that it's called electro!*

*Okay, fine, call it what you want*, she says, now taking her cellphone from her jeans pocket. *Rod Stewart okay with you ladies?* she asks, her eyes so bright that none of us think to contradict her.

Marguerite rolls her eyes and mumbles, *God, how corny. Seriously . . .*

The first distinctive notes of *Missing You* rise from the phone, immediately plunging the women into a kind of happy nostalgia.

Maud, pensive, draws invisible lines on the tablecloth with her knife, while Jeanne, staring into space, flashes a silly smile. Marguerite resists, nose wrinkled, but her sullen pout slowly loosens. Her body relaxes, swept along by the *corny* song's catchy melody in spite of herself. Her mother casts an imploring look in her direction. The young woman, seeming to immediately understand how to read that entreaty, stands up, a little grudgingly, and moving as decisively as her mother, fills the kettle with water.

I notice that the women always sing along with the same verse, softly, in unison: *"I ain't missing you at all . . ."* And without fail they stop at the same spot, letting the singer continue without them: *"I ain't missing you . . ."*

After that, there's no more talking, or very little. We drink our herbal tea, silent and peaceful. And the music is there to say what we don't say to one another.

The room is tiny, ten square feet, barely enough to hold a table and two chairs. On the ceiling, one bare bulb. The gray walls, dotted with flyspecks, smell of misery. There's not one window, not one air vent, not a single opening to the outside. The floor is warped linoleum covered with scuff marks. This individual visiting room is where I'm being made to wait. No way out. We're going to have to make do with limited space and, with no place for our eyes to wander, settle for staring at the walls.

The guards who escorted me here led me through an endless labyrinth of metallic doors, seven in all, which they systematically closed behind us in a chilling clatter. As I advanced, my breathing got shorter, as if every key twist, taking me a little farther from the outside world, was also depriving me of air. I sensed from the guards' cold looks that I wasn't welcome and that your quintuple murder had left a stink on me, like the decaying flesh of a corpse. Unless my confused mind twisted everything. After all, a guard has no reason to welcome people with a smile. He shares the same day-to-day as the men he guards.

I'm made to wait twenty minutes in the tiny room. I think of running away. Suddenly the door opens and a guard appears. His face is pale, thin; he looks sick. He asks me to follow him, tells me the warden of the correctional facility would like to speak to me. In a panic, I ask him why. He answers that he doesn't know. I know he knows, but he won't tell me anything. We repeat the labyrinth of corridors and the clatter of metallic doors. His back is wide and straight. He knows the way by heart, there's no hesitation in his step; he could walk it with his eyes closed.

When I enter the warden's office, he stands and holds out his hand. He is tall, big. I notice he's as pale as the guard. In his rush to sit back down, he bumps his knee against a table, reddens, and says, *Sorry, I never know where to put my legs.* His hands, placed on the table, do nothing. They tremble a little. His slightly bent fingers cling to an invisible handrail. I don't understand what I'm doing here, across from him, and the lost look in his eyes disconcerts me even more. He's the one to break the silence. His serious, even tone contrasts with the weakness in his hands. He says in one breath, as if to get rid of it, *I'm so very, very sorry to tell you that your partner died last night.*

Silence. His hands, abruptly, stop trembling. They unfurl slowly, flatten, finally breathe.

I turn my head toward the window, like my neck is being operated by an electric motor. Outside, there's a white sky.

*He's not my partner*, I reply. *He's no longer my partner.* And that's all I can think to say.

The warden doesn't know if he should congratulate me or console me.

He says, stumbling over the first words, *His heart . . . his heart stopped. We found him this morning . . . early. The doctor who usually treats him concluded it was a massive heart attack.*

I look at him, stunned. *The doctor who treats him?*

*Yes, your . . . Mr. Guillot developed a heart condition. You weren't aware?*

I shake my head no. He looks at me, surprised.

*We don't talk on the phone*, I clarify. *He would write to the girls every month. We had very limited contact.* Then I stop talking.

*I'm sure he wanted to spare you*, says the warden, hesitant.

*Maybe*, I respond. And I immediately think that if he had wanted to spare me, he wouldn't have died the day of my first visit.

The warden continues, *The doctor thinks it's highly likely that he was born with this particular condition. This kind of anomaly can reveal itself one day or remain dormant for an entire lifetime. There's no rule. There are people who live a healthy life and still develop it, and others who have terrible lifestyles and die in good health. It's a lottery. Mr. Guillot's illness manifested shortly after he was incarcerated. He was being monitored. He took medicine on a daily basis.*

Silence. I look at him again. I say, *How can you be sure that he was really taking it every day?*

The warden looks at his flattened hands, then says with a shrug, *We can't be sure, ma'am. We can't.*

At the end of the meeting, he tells me that he informed your parents and that they want to bring home your body for burial near where they live. He hands me a notebook.

*We found this under his pillow. It's yours now, if you want it.*

He walks me to the door and shakes my hand; his palm is damp.

In my hotel room, I fall asleep as soon as I lay my head on the pillow, in the middle of the day, for no reason. To take a break. To cease existing. After two or three hours of deep sleep, I start awake. I'm cold, terribly cold. I get up, grab my sweater from the back of the chair, immediately throw it on. Back in bed, I lean against the headboard and pull the quilt over my legs, my teeth chattering. I dreamed that you and I were making love. . . . And the indescribable pleasure making my heart beat faster troubles me all the more because I didn't expect to find the taste of your kisses still intact. Here you are, resurrected in my memory on the day of your death.

Tears rise. I don't hold them back. Am I crying from shame, exhaustion, grief? I have no idea and, ultimately, it doesn't matter anymore. At least it's that many less tears.

The sky grows overcast, the room suddenly plunges

into darkness. None of the sounds of the city reach me here. My breathing is calm. For a reason as strange as it is confusing, Marguerite's face invites itself into my innermost thoughts. Marguerite, her youth, her arrogance, her fierce will. But I'm not Marguerite—I had my day.

I'd placed your notebook on the nightstand. I open it slowly, as though I'm scared it will explode. Notes in your handwriting. Sentences really. Each one numbered. Like a list of groceries or tasks to be done. There are psalms, too, taken from the Bible; you cite them each time, in parentheses.

The prison warden told me that you'd been reading the Bible for some time, that you found comfort in it, especially David's psalms. At any other moment, I'd have found that ridiculous. You were never religious. But today it's different. I flip through your notebook and read a few of the psalms:

*"6:6. I am weary from groaning." (D. Psalm)*

*"3:1. How many rise up against me!" (D. Psalm)*

*"22:14. I am poured out like water, and all my bones are disjointed." (D. Psalm)*

*"7:15. He has dug a hole and hollowed it out; he has fallen into the pit of his making." (D. Psalm)*

*"6:7. My eyes fail from grief." (D. Psalm)*

*"20:8. We rise up and stand firm." (D. Psalm)*

*"22:6. But I am a worm and not a man." (D. Psalm)*

*"22:26. The poor will eat and be satisfied." (D. Psalm)*

*"26:2. Examine my heart and mind." (D. Psalm)*

*"31:12. I am like a broken vessel." (D. Psalm)*

I continue turning the pages of your notebook. I understand with a pang of emotion that it was your only company during these many months. On the last page, a sentence that you forgot to number, likely taken from David's psalms (since it's in quotes, too), grabs my attention:

*"I once was young and now am old."*

You underlined it with two thick strokes. You wanted it to be noticeable, and I did notice it. I read it and reread it, and though its simplicity troubles me, it also creates a feeling of familiarity. As if I'd written these words myself. I think they must have struck you the same way. As soothing as cool water. And that's no doubt the reason that they appear on the last page of your notebook, as if to bring an end to your reflections, to your quest, to your tragedy.

*"I once was young and now am old."*

In its great simplicity, this sentence says everything about us. Live, and then die. Rot. And the more I read it, the more I think that in reality you didn't forget to number it. You simply stripped it of its biblical coldness to make it something a man would say. You. And maybe that's what I came here looking for, just this. Like you did before me. Simple words worthy of man. And I understand now, in light of this silence you've left behind you, what your lawyer was trying to say, the day of his closing argument, when he cited Voltaire. He had said, after taking a long breath: *"One can be more criminal than one knows."** It seems obvious now that he was addressing everyone in the courtroom, from the simple spectators to the judge, everyone, including himself, like he was flinging mud in our faces.

I don't know if we're all capable of killing with as much as savagery as you had. I still don't understand where it could have come from. That mystery will prob-

*Voltaire, *Oedipus: A Play in Five Acts*, trans. Frank J. Morlock (Cabin John, MD: Wildside Press, 2012).

ably haunt me until the end. What I do know, how-ever, is that no one around you was innocent. We stood back and let it happen. Like a chain reaction, each of us contributed to an outcome. A horrific act. A tragedy. Our tragedy. I also tell myself that maybe there were words that would have kept you from sinking, except we didn't even know that we were losing you; we hadn't understood that yet.

Behind the window, the sun pierces through two clouds. For the first time in a long time I think about Bakary. His memory awakens others: the gentle valley, the burning thatch, the pine resin perfuming the air, the whispers of summer, at night, beneath the white moon.... A flood of smells and feelings. I choke back a sob.

There's stamping above my room, furniture being moved, a slamming door. Certainly the maid. The smell of omelets and fried mushrooms rises up the stairs. Maybe the proprietor will come knock on my door soon, invite me to her table, gesturing with her small hands. I'll agree to join them, because today those women are the only people I have. We'll laugh, and then Jeanne will go back to her room for a short nap. The proprietor will refuse our help clearing the table, and tonight we'll drink to our health. And tomorrow morning, when I tell them goodbye, all of them, and they respond with *See you next time*, I won't ruin anything. I'll hug the proprietor last, because you always save the best for last, and I'll tell her, *See you next time,* too, with the same warmth in my voice, the same kindness in my eyes, the same trembling humanity.

## *Author's Note*

Perhaps the most fascinating thing about headline-grabbing stories—think "true crime"—is their power to connect us. They get us talking, but also reading. Whenever a scandal or a crime makes the news, people concoct hypotheses, discuss, take sides, and argue, until the mystery is solved and order restored.

Restore order. That's what authors try to do as well, albeit in a very specific way. As Roland Barthes suggests, the incidents that capture our attention—the infamous *faits divers*, as the French call them—defy neat categorization; they "begin to exist only where the world stops being named."* Literature fills in those blanks, naming the unnameable. It dwells in darkness and tries to bring forth light. The writer doesn't take the place of justice; that's not their role. They mustn't judge, or choose a side, or even presume to deliver justice. They offer one version—theirs—and attempt to get closer to the shadows.

*People Like Them* is loosely inspired by a mass homicide committed in 2003 in a village in France's Haute-Savoie region. At the time it made headlines, no news articles or radio or television shows mentioned any racist motives. Or at least I can't remember any that did. Why such an omission? I still can't figure it out. The refusal to take into consideration one of the essential keys to understanding that tragedy is incomprehensible. I'm not saying that racism is the only factor that drove the murderer to kill a family of five—it's infinitely more complex than that—but it quickly became clear in my mind that the father's skin color must have played a decisive role.

In my novel, Bakary's powerful charisma, as well as his social status, drives Constant mad with jealousy. In

*Roland Barthes, "Structure of the *Fait-Divers*," *Critical Essays*, trans. Richard Howard (Evanston, IL: Northwestern University Press, 1972), 185.

Constant's mind, the normal order (an order that persists in the collective unconscious) has been altered—reversed, in fact. The Black man is powerful while the white man has been diminished, both physically and socially. This reversal of roles is intolerable to Constant because it doesn't correspond to anything he knows. In an attempt to restore order—a notion that keeps coming back—he murders Bakary. Sylvia and the children, viewed by Constant as an extension of Bakary, aren't spared.

The casual racism at play here is invisible and insidious. It's not outright, it doesn't look you straight in the eyes; this racism only reveals itself obliquely (e.g., stereotypes, inappropriate remarks, clumsy comments). The phenomenon is all the more paradoxical given that there's not a single foreigner in Carmac. The villagers' fears and speculations are fed by the media-propagated specter of a foreign threat. Oftentimes, in these villages "protected" from invasion by outsiders, people end up fighting invisible enemies and defending themselves from abstractions.

I wasn't entirely faithful to the facts. The news story in question was primarily a reference point. I kept the quintuple murder, the friendship between the two men, the clash of two social classes, the hiring of the murderer's wife as a housecleaner by their neighbors, and the financial scam. All the rest is fictional.

Constant has nothing. He could have had everything, but life decided otherwise. His career as a great athlete ended abruptly, leaving him physically impaired and robbed of a bright future. He is a weakened man. A shell of a man. The arrival of Bakary—a man who does have everything: money, happiness, health—disrupts Constant's entire existence. At first, their friendship boosts his self-esteem, but when that relationship is marred by betrayal, Constant feels such humiliation that his only response is to eliminate those he considers responsible for his unbearable suffering.

When you dive into the murky waters of a true story, some self-searching is also involved. Class relations have always fascinated me. I come from a family of very modest means and was forced to deal with social injustice from an early age. I witnessed my own parents' distress as they confronted daily humiliations and the lack of steady employment. Later, in adulthood, on the heels of a rich acting career, I was compelled by financial reasons to clean people's homes. I was forty-four years old and I hadn't planned on going backward. I was never ashamed of having grown up in the milieu I come from, but, like everyone, I wanted to move onward and upward. For that matter, I was raised to strive to "do better." Our parents repeated that constantly: "Do better than us!"

I cleaned houses for three years. What sticks in my mind about that strange and painful experience is a certain look. A look that doesn't register your presence. As if the person doesn't see you, or your outlines are blurry. A look that makes you invisible and that, from the start, defines you as "worthless." That look was different in every way from how I had always been regarded in my career as an actress. Actors are loved, admired, and envied. You don't elicit the same reaction when you're a housecleaner. You abruptly go from everything to nothing, from visible to invisible, for the simple reason that you no longer hold the same job. Everything that makes you who you are gets downgraded—absolutely everything. This happens because we exist in a brutal society whose sole reigning values are work and money. And yet nothing inside you has really changed.

That experience—a drop in social standing, humiliation, distrust (often involuntary) from employers—helped shape the characters of Anna and Constant. Everything has been set up to grind them down.

I don't judge my characters, nor do I intend to condemn them. Criminals—even murderers—serve as mirror images; they reflect our own fallibility. Viewing them as monstrous aberrations prevents us from understanding human nature. There's no such thing as monsters. Only humans.